THE FRINGE SERIES

"Best science fiction I have read in a long while."
  ~Michael D. Griffiths, *SF Reader*

"*Fringe Runner* is epic fun with great characters, action, and suspense. Rachel Aukes is the next big name in the Space Opera genre!"
  ~ Nicholas Sansbury Smith, best-selling author of the *Extinction Cycle* series

"A perfect read for fans of the fantasy and sci-fi genres."
  ~ Ethan Gregory, *One Guy's Guide to Good Reads*

"I would recommend this novel to anyone who likes action-filled space operas and stories about fighting against the ruling government."
  ~ *Audiobook Reviewer*

EARTH UNDER SIEGE

"...Everything I've come to expect from this author. It's packed full of action, drama, surprise and suspense at every turn."
  ~Silvia at *Goodreads*

"Highly Recommended. Five Mysterious Stars."
  ~*RBS Productions*

"A top ten book!"
  ~ *Step into Fiction*

FRINGE CAMPAIGN

Waymaker Wars

Space Troopers

Flight of the Javelin

Bounty Hunter

Fringe Series

The Deadland Saga

FRINGE CAMPAIGN

FRINGE SERIES
BOOK 3

RACHEL AUKES

FRINGE CAMPAIGN

Edited by Riva Reading and Kriegler Editing Services
Cover art © Vivid Covers | www.VividCovers.com

2nd edition 2022

ISBN: 978-0-9899018-8-8

For Brian, always.

CONTENTS

CHAPTER 1

RECLAIMING REBUS

Rebus Station, Terra
Critch

CRITCH SCANNED the building across the street through his binoculars.

"Are they set up yet?" Birk asked at Critch's side on the warehouse roof.

"Not yet. They're running late. Lucky for them, Seda's also running late. Can't anything get done on time around here?"

"Looks like our friends in the Collective Unified Forces are right on schedule," Birk said. "Seventeen minutes after the motion sensors were triggered."

Critch glanced down to see a patrol car turn onto the street below. He scowled and looked back across the street. Still no sign of his other team.

"What do we do?" his right-hand man asked.

He read his wrist comm. No update from Seda Faulk. If Critch moved now, the stationmaster could be on his own. If Critch waited, they'd blow their chance at taking the warehouse district. He put away his binoculars, and then motioned to the team waiting behind him on the roof. "Showtime."

He heard footsteps as his team took off running across the roof to move into positions on the lower floors.

Birk lifted the portable photon cannon and rested it on the roof's edge. He took his time as he aimed at the patrol car.

Critch waited and watched in perfect stillness. Inside, his heart raced. Adrenaline was pulsing through every muscle, and he was ready to leap up at any second.

Birk fired. The beam hit the patrol car in the center. The vehicle exploded in beautiful blue and orange flames. Death to the occupants would've been instantaneous.

Critch leapt to his feet and helped Birk strap the large cannon onto his back. They ran across the roof. When they reached the door, he checked the time. They had roughly thirty-eight seconds before the gunships would arrive, and another six minutes before military vans would arrive.

Birk was first through the door, with Critch right behind him. They hustled down the stairs, all nine flights, until they reached the ground floor. The increasing sounds of loud engines rattled the windows. As a pair of gunships approached the district, Critch and Birk dove under a waterbed that had been propped up on two-by-fours.

Critch check his comm. Thirty-nine seconds. *Not bad.*

The gunships all but skimmed the buildings as they scanned for heat signatures. When the planes didn't fire, Critch felt himself relax ever so slightly. He knew then that his teams had all reached their positions in time, hiding under waterbeds to camouflage their body heat.

When the gunships swooped in for a second pass, cannon fire blasted upward from windows in the warehouse across the street. Critch rolled out from under the camouflage to see the first gunship explode. The second gunship lost a wing, and it spiraled into the ground, exploding upon impact. Windows shattered, and Critch shielded his face from flying glass shards.

He shook his head at the CUF's obstinate adherence to standard operating procedures. He knew gunships always flew two passes to scan for heat signatures. The CUF likely assumed insurgents would move after the first pass, that their targets would think they were then safe. What the CUF didn't assume was that torrents had studied the military's routines. The first pass gave Critch's teams time to acquire moving targets in their automated sights, and the second pass gave them the opportunity to produce an impressive fireworks display.

More gunships would come, but Critch knew the CUF kept only two ships on standby. By the time they finally got around to sending more, the vanloads of dromadiers would already be deployed and in the middle of a maelstrom.

He checked his wrist comm. *Eight minutes.* He tapped it to open his team's channel. "Be ready for ducks in eight."

Birk moved to the window, where two old style rifles were propped. He brushed off broken glass, picked up both weapons, and handed one to Critch.

Critch checked the gun to make sure the explosion hadn't damaged it. Satisfied, he gave Birk a nod. "Stay low. For some reason, Throttle likes that ugly mug of yours."

"Your mug is so ugly a vig would run squealing from you," Birk replied drily.

Critch grinned and turned from Birk, and jogged across the warehouse floor. The spot he'd picked earlier was now blocked by the burning tail of a gunship, and so he went a few windows down. He moved into position and waited. He checked his comm every few seconds. When it was time, he reported out, "Ducks in two. Eyes peeled."

Critch hated waiting, but so much of every battle was waiting, with short bursts of insane chaos. He felt at home in the chaos, when everything was reflexive, when he didn't have time to think or second-guess himself. It was the time *after* the battle he hated most, when his mind replayed snapshots, and the second-guessing began. Not that he'd ever admit to others that such thoughts crossed his mind. To the torrent army, he was scar-faced Drake Fender, fearless torrent marshal and cold-blooded killer. His unwavering drive gave them confidence. And if the torrents were to have a shot at taking Rebus Station, they needed every bit of confidence they could get.

He heard the vans before he saw them cut through the smoky street. The CUF had sent three vans this time. Three squads of droms.

"Sitting ducks," Critch announced into his wrist comm. He took a step back from the window, settled down on a knee, and adjusted his scope on the first van coming to a stop outside.

The droms poured out of the vans, using long clear shields as protection. The shields were designed to ward off photon blasts, and could hold up against small caliber gunfire. Today would be the first time the droms on Terra would experience fire from sniper rifles.

He found his target. His finger moved to the trigger. A drom to the right of his target fell, and the others looked around, confused. The gunshot had come from Critch's side. *Birk.* Critch didn't fire yet. Instead, he waited until he slowly exhaled before he pulled the trigger. His target went down immediately.

He moved to his next target. By now, the remaining droms realized their shields and body armor weren't protecting them, and they ran for cover. Critch kept his breath steady and smoothly tracked his running target. He fired, and another drom fell.

By the time he'd made his third kill, there were no more easy marks. The remaining soldiers had found cover and were now returning fire. Critch reloaded. Unable to find a target, he ran through the warehouse to get a better angle. He saw Birk was taking fire, and so he rushed up to a window to find the source.

There.

Two droms were firing nonstop photon blasts from the warehouse across the street. Critch squinted and then lined up his sight on a drom's shoulder. The round would likely result in a wound rather than a kill, but if he didn't take the shot, the droms would hit Birk out of sheer quantity of blasts, rather than by skill.

He fired. The drom disappeared behind the wall. Then a barrage of return fire came in Critch's direction. He dropped to the floor, grunting when he landed hard on his rifle.

The sounds of engines drowned out the gunfire, and Critch scowled. He'd planned to have the three squads taken care of before more ships arrived. Their odds had suddenly dropped. He heard the gunships fire, and he wondered if the pilots knew if they were firing at torrents or at their own droms.

Critch was safe from heat-sensors as long the photon blasts cooked up the area around him enough to make sweat run down his face and back.

He tapped his wrist comm to make the call for backup.

Hari's visage appeared. "You ready for me?"

"It's getting hot down here," he yelled.

"On my way. I'll be there to cool things down in thirty seconds."

He disconnected, and crawled across the floor to get away from the gunfire. The droms kept firing nonstop at any target they could zero in on. The thing about photon fire was, they could fire at a building long enough to burn a hole through a wall to get to the target on the other side. He was lucky the warehouse was built with stone blocks, which meant the wall would hold longer than most.

Critch had chosen sniper rifles for this battle rather than photon guns to penetrate CUF shielding. The downside of using rifles was, they had a limited supply of ammunition on hand, which meant they had to take their time to aim. He patted his photon gun, ready to pull it out. But it was only a handgun, with a fraction of a photon rifle's energy that the droms outside were using.

Birk's cannon fired to his right, and the barrage that had been raining in Critch's direction was suddenly gone. He took a risk and looked out to see that where the two droms had been under cover was now a large hole in the warehouse wall. He stood and ran over to Birk's location.

"Thanks for drawing their fire," Birk said.

"Anytime," Critch muttered before patting the younger man on the back. His comm chimed, and he read the message. "Seda's through."

Birk nodded.

A high-pitched engine screamed as *Razor's Edge* dived at the CUF gunships.

"Hari's crashed the party," Critch said.

Birk blew out a breath. "About time."

Critch looked out the window as the gunships broke off from their strafing runs to go after the new threat. *Razor's Edge* dwarfed the two gunships, which were more agile but had far less speed and firepower.

He turned his attention back to the ground. The battle had calmed down, with only one source of active photon fire remaining.

"I want that drom alive," Critch announced through his comm.

Critch, Birk, and the two teams converged on the remaining dromadier. An explosion from behind them shook the ground. The men ducked for cover while Critch pivoted to locate the source of the blast. Billowing black smoke drew his vision upward. It appeared that Hari had taken out one gunship. The second had chosen discretion over honor and was hightailing it out of the area.

Hari wagged her wings as she flew over the warehouse district before disappearing into the distance.

The rest of Critch's first team caught up with him and Birk on the ground floor. They crossed the street as a single unit, moving quickly yet warily toward the second team, who had their rifles leveled on a drom kneeling before them.

Critch stepped up to the soldier. He was young, likely on his first tour. He bore normal white skin, meaning he could've been from Alluvia or any colony.

"Where are you from?" Critch demanded.

The man pursed his lips and didn't speak.

"Alluvian. I thought so. Well, it's your lucky day, citizen. You get to live."

The man's eyes darted to Critch in surprise.

Critch nodded. "You are to report to your superiors that the warehouse district has been reclaimed by Terrans. Only colonists are free to pass through here."

"Is—is that all?" the man asked.

"You want more?" Critch countered. "Okay. Tell them that for every colonist they kill on Terra, we'll kill two citizens."

The drom's eyes grew wide.

Critch motioned for the man to stand. "You'd better get up and hustle back to your commander before I change my mind."

The drom came shakily to his feet. He kept his hands behind his head and his eyes focused on Critch as he backed away slowly. After he'd gone several feet, he turned and started running down the street.

Birk chuckled. "I never get tired of seeing a citizen piss his pants."

Critch continued to watch the soldier until he disappeared around the corner.

"This was a big day. We're one neighborhood closer to the docks," Nat said off to Critch's right.

"We could lose it tomorrow if we're not careful." Critch looked to the sky. "Let's get under cover. I don't trust the CUF to be smart enough to know when they've sent in enough young folks to die for one day."

He knew the CUF could bomb these buildings, but they were still trying to portray themselves as the defenders rather than the aggressors. Bombed-out buildings tended to look bad on the news. The Collective still controlled the media, but more and more reporters were reporting the truth, causing contradictory stories and confusion as to what was accurate.

Thanks to conflicting news stories and Seda's proclamations, the CUF was losing face in the public eye, which meant they may be forced to go further to regain control. He suspected the CUF was only weeks, if not days, away from starting bombing runs.

Critch left one team at the warehouse district to collect weapons and set up a lookout station. He took his second team back to their headquarters at Seda Faulk's hidden retreat.

Seda stood by the hangar door when they arrived. The stationmaster grinned. "Now, that was some diversion. I could see the battle from orbit. Needless to say, we broke orbit and made it here without a single eye on us."

"You're lucky you weren't later. The party was almost over before you arrived."

"But, it wasn't." Seda nodded in the direction of where the battle had taken place. "How'd it go?"

"We have the warehouse district," Critch said.

"Casualties?"

Critch shook his head. "None. First time for that. I think they're running low on experienced droms on Terra."

Seda sobered. "They'll send down more. They aren't willing to give up Rebus Station, not with the juice plants here. Speaking of which, did you know Parliament is trying to push through an act to claim all Faulk Industries holdings? They said that since I'm an enemy of the state, all my business holdings should become property of the Collective."

Critch narrowed his gaze. "If they go after your businesses, they'd have every juice plant on Terra."

Seda chuckled. "Oh, they can try."

Critch then noticed Jeyde Sixx in the hangar, looking the worse for wear. He frowned when the usually social thief kept walking without acknowledging the group. "I take it the trip wasn't a total success."

"No. Every trail Sixx followed led to a contradictory trail. As for what I learned..." He got a faraway look before turning a hard gaze upon Critch. "Mason killed Mariner. He has full control of the Founders, at least what's left of them."

Critch's lips parted. Mason—the alias Gabriel Heid used within the secret organization—killed as smoothly as a glass of Terran whiskey. Mason had played a hand in the creation of the blight, which had killed thousands, though the death Critch took most personally was that of Demes, the youngest member of Critch's crew.

"I'm sorry," Critch said. "I know she was your wife."

Seda seemed surprised Critch knew, but he shook it off. "That doesn't matter right now. What matters is that I learned Mason didn't just execute her; he tortured her for information, no doubt, information specifically about me."

"How much do you think she told him?"

Seda grimaced. "Everything."

Devil Town, Spate
Reyne

"ALL SYSTEMS GREEN. Let's hope your intel is still good," Throttle said from the *Gryphon*'s pilot seat. Her hands tapped across the instrument panel as the ship broke Spate's atmosphere and made its descent to Devil Town's space dock.

"It'd better be, or this trip will be very short," Captain Aramis Reyne said as he scanned the brown sky for any signs of patrol ships planetside. That the CUF patrols in orbit were light was reassuring—so far, everything was exactly as the latest intel provided on CUF operations in the Spate sector. The CUF had focused its armada around Terra, where the Fringe Liberation Campaign was in full swing, but with martial law deployed across the fringe, traveling from planet to planet without drawing unwanted attention had become complicated. He thought for a moment, then tacked on, "Better be ready for a hasty retreat, just in case."

"Just in case," she echoed.

Turbulence bumped the ship around as it descended through the planet's thin atmosphere, and the gravity pulled at the *Gryphon* like it'd been weighted down with lead. The young pilot handled the controls deftly, entering minute directional changes to minimize atmo burn.

"Here comes the moment of truth. Let's see if Devil Town is still an equal opportunity colony," she said before transmitting. "Dock Control, this is Phantom Cruiser Specter-Seven-Five-Five-One-Bravo. Request approval for docking sequence."

"Phantom Five-One-Bravo, docking approved. Proceed to Dock Hilo-Two. Notice to airmen, Docks Alpha through Charlie are in use by the Collective Unified Forces."

Throttle exhaled. "Sweet Sabra, the docks are still under Spaten control."

Reyne could see the tension relax from Throttle's shoulders, but he didn't share her relief. The CUF was using three docks, each with twenty slips, which meant there could be up to sixty ships docked at Devil Town. He may have drastically underestimated how many dromadiers were patrolling the fringe station. *Too many.*

Throttle replied to the dock control operator. "Phantom Five-One-Bravo acknowledged. Thanks for the notice. Proceeding to Dock Hilo-Two."

The *Gryphon* broke through the cloud layer, and the space dock came into view.

Reyne tapped the ship's comm. "Boden, prepare for docking."

"Aye, aye, Captain," came the mechanic's reply.

As Throttle ran the ship through its docking procedures, Reyne found his attention drawn to the larger docks, where the CUF ships sat, and he had to remind himself that no one on the ground could see the torrent symbol—the outline of a teardrop—painted on the side of his ship.

Dock Hilo was the smallest of the docks, and set apart from

the other docks for privacy. Hilo was generally reserved for private ships and the colony's elite customers—the wealthy or famous who didn't want to be seen or have to walk through the crowds on the main docks. Recently, thanks to a generously large contribution to the dock control station operators, Hilo had been set aside for use by torrent ships. The CUF had no idea enemy ships were docking mere kilometers away from their own ships.

Throttle settled the *Gryphon* into its landing bay as gently as a mother placing her baby in a crib. Next to them sat the *Nighthawk*, a pirate ship with the torrent teardrop emblazoned across its side.

Throttle's brow rose. "If Five B's wanted to make a statement, I think he did. The CUF could've seen that paint job from a hundred miles away."

Humor tugged at Reyne's lip as he remembered the last time he drank with the *Nighthawk*'s captain—he'd yet to drink with Five B's and *not* end up in the middle of a brawl. "It's Five B's. For some reason, I'm not surprised." He thought for a moment. "It's good news for us. No CUF patrols have come through this dock, or else the *Nighthawk* would have been publicly demolished by now."

"Let's hope it stays that way," Throttle said.

The constant thrum of the *Gryphon* fell silent as Throttle shut down the ship's systems. Reyne unbuckled from his seat and pushed to his feet. His arthritic joints protested the quick movement after sitting for several hours. He clenched his jaw to hide any outward sign of pain.

"Did you take a pill today?" Throttle asked.

Reyne grimaced. His daughter knew him too well. "I'll pick up more on the way back from Gin's."

She unlocked her wheelchair and pushed back from the instrument panel. "You'd better. I'll have the *Gryph* refueled and ready to go by the time you get back." She tacked on, "I don't like hanging around this close to the CUF, so try not to window-shop, okay?"

"Trust me, I don't plan to hang out in Devil Town any longer than I have to."

Throttle chuckled. "That'd be a different story if Sixx were along. He'd have us on the ground for half a day while he caught up with all his old girlfriends."

Reyne's grin faded when he thought of his friend. The handsome kleptomaniac was a personal favorite of Devil Town's red-light district. But Sixx had changed when he'd learned his wife could still be alive. He'd become obsessed with finding her to the point of leaving Reyne's crew to join Seda on a trip to Myr to find her.

He clasped Throttle's shoulder. "Keep an eye out for trouble. At the first sign of dromadiers, head to Gin's. With the new order to destroy every torrent ship on sight, the last place you'll want to be is on board this ship if it falls into CUF hands."

"Aye, aye Captain Obvious," she said wryly, and then wheeled off the bridge.

Reyne sighed and headed to his bunk to grab the satchel he needed to deliver, and to load up on extra weapons and credits. Devil Town had a knack for offering surprises, and Reyne couldn't be too prepared. When he stepped into the hallway, Boden was already there, armed comparably to Reyne, with two photon guns in a chest holster and two knives strapped to his belt.

Reyne patted the bag he'd slung across his shoulders. "It'll be a quick in-and-out. Just a drop-off and then back to Playa." He paused to give his mechanic a once-over. "You ready for this?"

Boden's lips thinned. "I'm good."

They both knew Reyne's question had nothing to do with Boden being prepared for their mission, and everything to do with Boden being a recovering sweet soy addict about to step foot into the galaxy's sweet soy capital.

"You'd better be. Without Sixx, I'm counting on you."

"I won't let you down," he said quickly.

The older man wanted to believe Boden. "Okay. Let's head out. Throttle gave us strict orders to get back fast, and I don't want to be on her bad side."

Boden chuckled. "Me neither. I'd better say goodbye." He started to head to her bunk.

"She's already outside with dock control to refuel the ship."

"Oh," Boden stopped, a tinge of disappointment in his voice.

Boden had saved Reyne's life more than once, but the mechanic also had more than one personality flaw. One of them was his warm-and-cold treatment of Throttle. She had feelings for the handsome Alluvian, and he had feelings for her...sometimes. Other times, when he was deep into the sweet soy, he barely acknowledged her existence. For the past few months, he'd been openly flirting with her. Reyne suspected the display of affection had something to do with Birk, a member of Critch's crew, who spent every planetside leave—and even the occasional spaceside rendezvous—with her.

The only thing Reyne cared about was that lately, she'd been the happiest he remembered.

Reyne grabbed two breather masks and handed one to Boden. They headed off the ship, down the ramp, and onto the dock's composite walkways.

As they traversed the ramp, Reyne noticed several cargo ships brandishing the blue crest of Myr. The colony, currently absent a stationmaster, was a wildcard. While the CUF had established martial law on Spate, the Collective had not yet assigned a new stationmaster. He suspected the delay came from the Fringe Liberation Campaign distracting Parliament. Regardless of the reason, no stationmaster was good news for Reyne. The colony would be too volatile for any Myrad or Alluvian businessmen to be approved to come here on their own. At least, that's what Reyne figured. These ships posed a quandary. "Maybe the economy's worse than I thought," he said to himself.

"What's that?" Boden asked.

"Nothing really," he replied. "I'm surprised at seeing Myrad haulers here. There's no way insurance would cover their ships and cargo on Spate right now. Not without a stationmaster in place."

"I guess the Myrad recession is bad enough for some citizens to buck the odds in coming here for trade," Boden said.

"I suppose so." Reyne remained dubious.

They strolled past the Myrad ships without any outward signs of stress. Inside, Reyne's every muscle was taut as he constantly scanned for dromadiers.

Since Reyne's old, black mug topped every CUF's most-wanted list, he was thankful the breather mask hid his face. Boden was unknown to the CUF, but being an Alluvian, he tended to stick out in the colonies, so the breather masks benefited both men.

Once they were safely clear of the docks, the tension eased slightly from Reyne's shoulders. They could blend into the multitudes of people in Devil Town, Spate's largest colony and the only one with a fringe station. They stood on a corner while Boden tapped his wrist comm to hail a cab.

Something nudged the back of Reyne's leg. He spun around to find a scrawny vig trying to eat through his boot. He kicked it, and it went flying for several feet with a squeal.

"Damn rodents," Reyne muttered. Vigs were everywhere on Spate, and would eat anything. They looked like a cross between a rat and a small pig, minus the hair. And they tasted *awful*. For being carbon-based life-forms, one would think they'd taste better. Vigs were originally created to be food for colonists, but instead, they were the ultimate example of how biome kits didn't always establish biological colonies as expected.

A cab pulled up and an older woman stepped out. She tugged on a leash, and a wombie stumbled out, carrying her luggage. Reyne cringed at seeing a human treated in such a fashion, but the wombie—a Spaten mutant—didn't seem the least bothered.

Spate was the Collective's largest producer of blue tea, a drink that enabled humans to survive on far less water than normal. It had enabled colonies on desolate rocks to thrive, and it reduced the water cargo weight in space travel, making room for more food, which meant much greater distances.

Blue tea didn't come without costs. The second-generation humans whose parents survived only on blue tea were born with reduced intelligence. After several generations, those who subsisted off blue tea developed physical mutations as well. Small bumps for storing water appeared on their bodies, similar to the humps camels on Earth developed. These colonists' intelligence had degraded enough that they were no longer referred to as colonists. Instead, they'd become water-deficient zombies, or wombies, good for manual labor and not much else.

Every planet had changed its colonists in unique ways. On Reyne's home planet of Playa, those who embraced the planet's low gravity for generations produced stretches. Myrads all had bluish skin from severe argyria due to the massive amounts of silver found everywhere on the planet.

Reyne leaned back in his seat while Boden entered their destination in the automated cab system. The cab had breathable air, but the pair left their masks on to avoid being scanned by the facial recognition system Reyne knew was installed in every cab in the Collective.

Neither spoke due to the likelihood the cab was also running a voice recognition program. Spate had remained relatively free of CUF oversight until the past year. Reyne had been one of the masterminds behind the Fringe Liberation Campaign—a rebellion against the oppressive control and taxation by the Collective that was run by the system's two founding planets, Myr and Alluvia.

Reyne had expected the CUF to come down hard on the torrents on Terra, where the Campaign was taking place. He hadn't expected colonists to rise up across the fringe and join the cause. Protests had erupted in every large colony, and one-off attacks against dromadiers became daily news. In response, the CUF initiated martial law across all colonies in the Collective, attempting to quell the rebellion by putting the colonists in a stranglehold.

The CUF had never understood the colonies' power, and they were about to find out just how strong the colonies had become.

He gazed out the window as the cab drove them to the grittier downtown area of Devil Town, where the red-light district stood. Built to replicate an old Earth scene, strippers danced in windows, and prostitutes stood outside trying to woo passersby into their brothel.

At the end of the district, a three-story mansion stood over the red-light district like a stern father watching over his unruly children. Reyne found humor in the thought, as the comparison wasn't far from the truth. Gin James was Devil Town's wealthiest pimp now that Lincoln Finn was out of the picture. Everyone assumed he'd become Devil Town's next stationmaster, but he had yet to publicly side with the CUF or the torrents. Reyne had traveled to Spate to gain Gin's support through money. And lots of it.

The cab's whirring engine slowed as the vehicle pulled to a stop outside Gin's estate.

Reyne looked at the front yard and grimaced.

Boden broke the silence. "Is that..."

"Yeah," Reyne said. "Ah, hell."

Gin was in his front yard. He hung from a noose a few feet above the ground. By the looks of his purple, puffy face and bulging eyes, he'd hung there for at least a day. Since Spate's air had negligible levels of oxygen and carbon, the easiest way to kill someone was to lock them outside without a breather mask. Someone was clearly making a statement in Gin's case.

Reyne noticed the execution order posted near the body:

This colonist has been found guilty of disobedience and has been sentenced to hang by the neck until dead. Sentence to be carried out immediately upon the order of Stationmaster Axos Wintsel.

His body went cold. *Wintsel.*

"Wintsel? Hey, isn't that—"

"Get us back to the docks now," Reyne said. There was no way the name was a coincidence.

An alarm in the cab sounded. Both tried to open the doors to no avail.

"The vehicle is under lockdown. Remain calm until the lockdown has concluded," the cab's voice system announced.

"We've got droms," Boden said.

Reyne looked in the direction of Boden's focus and saw a squad headed toward them. He pulled out his gun and blasted the door several times before it fell outward. Reyne jumped outside, quickly followed by Boden.

Reyne pointed. "Alley!"

They took off running. The door they'd escaped through was on the opposite side of the cab to the incoming dromadiers, so the soldiers didn't notice anything until Reyne and Boden sprinted out beyond the cab.

"Stop!" someone yelled, though the command was somewhat muffled through his mask.

Neither man slowed down. Photon blasts pounded the ground around them. Reyne shielded his face from debris kicking up from the street.

Boden reached the alley first and was opening a door by the time Reyne caught up. They ran inside and locked the door behind them. They turned to find a woman wearing nothing but a bustier and thong, and incredibly high heels. She gave Boden an appraising look. Her sultry smile hinted her approval of what she saw.

"Is there another exit?" Boden asked.

Her brows rose. "Why would you want to leave? We haven't even met yet."

Reyne fished out a hundred-credit and tossed it to her.

She caught it with a deft hand. Her expression turned all business, and she nodded to the hallway behind her. "Turn right at the end of the hall. Through the kitchen."

They took off down the hallway when a pounding on the back door ensued.

"CUF. Let us in!"

Reyne glanced back briefly to see the woman saunter ever so slowly toward the back door. She looked over her shoulder long enough to give Reyne a wink, and he gave her a small nod. Her delay would buy them a few seconds, though he suspected it wouldn't be enough.

The other door was exactly where she'd said it would be, and they barreled through the doorway and found themselves in another alley. They ran onto a side street and down the sidewalk, which was nearly empty of pedestrians, making it impossible for them to blend into a crowd.

Boden was faster, and began to put distance between them. Reyne bit through the pain in his joints and pushed himself to keep up with the Alluvian one-third his age. Boden continued leading them down streets and through alleys as though winding them through a maze. He ran into a diminutive grocery store, and Reyne followed, panting.

Boden put both hands on the counter and spoke quietly to the clerk. "I'm looking for a 2720-year Terran whiskey."

The clerk nodded. His hand slipped under the counter, and the back door of the small store opened.

Boden motioned for Reyne to follow, and the mechanic headed through the back doorway, which led them to a dark stairway.

As they descended, Reyne said, "I'm curious. The Terrans didn't start making whiskey until 2725."

"This place isn't technically legal," Boden replied. "Which means we should be safe here until the droms quit looking for us."

Reyne frowned. If Boden was familiar with this place, then it wasn't much safer than being on the streets.

He really could've used Sixx on this mission. His friend knew every brothel around Devil Town. Where Boden turned to drugs to escape his problems, Sixx turned to companionship.

At the bottom of the stairs, a short woman stood in the dim light. She was nearly as round as she was tall. A dozen chaises lined the walls. Several beds had occupants lounging as though boneless. The sweetness to the air left no doubt in Reyne's mind they'd entered a sweet soy lounge. The last place Boden should be.

The woman scowled. "There's a hefty surcharge for bringing droms to my store."

"We lost them a couple blocks back," Boden said.

She guffawed. "There's a camera on every corner of every

street. They'll see you entered my store but never left. There will be a squad here in under five minutes." She walked over to a comm panel on the wall. "Luis, you're about to have company looking for our customers. Take care of it."

"You got it, Mother."

The woman turned back to Reyne and Boden. "Off with your masks. Let me get a good look at my customers."

They complied.

Boden spoke first. "I'm not here to buy."

Her lips pursed. "Tsk, tsk. Only customers are allowed in my den."

Reyne stepped in, and the woman narrowed her gaze upon him. "We just need somewhere to burn a few minutes," he said. "We're happy to compensate you for the inconvenience."

"Oh, you'll do that," she replied and cocked her head. "It's not every day a leader of the torrent rebellion ends up in my quaint store."

She turned to Boden. "And I remember you. It's been a while. But I never forget a customer, especially when that customer is a citizen. We don't get many citizens in Devil Town. And you've been here more than once, because I have the best sweet soy around. If you're not here for it now, then there's no reason for you to stay."

Reyne reached into his pocket and fished out several large credits. He dropped them into her open palm. When she kept it open, he gave her several more. She hefted the weight in her hand as though she were considering if it was enough.

"I'm Madame Grecklin. Welcome to my shop," she said with a broad smile. "By now, my son will have fed images of you running from my shop and into my competitor's shop down the block. Now, of course, if they know they're looking for Aramis Reyne, then they won't give up the search."

"They don't know my identity," Reyne corrected. "We never

took off our masks, and didn't speak enough for voice patterns to be analyzed."

"Then, the streets should be clear for you within three hours. There are plenty of other criminals for the droms to chase around here," she said. "Until then, sit back, relax, and enjoy yourselves. Feel free to partake in my special treats. Guaranteed to quench even the sweetest sweet tooth."

On her way out, she brushed against Boden and conspicuously slipped a bag of sweet soy in his pocket. He visibly tensed. She patted his thigh. "For later," she said and left through a side door.

Boden scowled. He pulled out the bag, emotion flashed through his eyes as he eyed it for a second, and then he tossed it onto the chest of a man currently entranced in a soy haze. Without a word, he strode to a chaise in the farthest corner from the addicts in the lounge, plopped down, and laid an arm over his eyes.

Reyne knew his mechanic was waging a battle to not give in to his addiction. He took the seat nearest Boden so he could keep watch over his crewmember. When Boden didn't stir, Reyne turned his focus to his wrist comm. He called Throttle, but there was no answer. He tried again. After the third unanswered call, he left a message. "Throttle, there's a new stationmaster who's not friendly. Chances are, the CUF are on their way to the docks, so take off. Do not wait for us. We'll catch another lift and will rendezvous with you at Alpha."

He hung up and sighed, hoping she'd get the message in time. By now, the CUF would have pulled the cab's records and know that the two men had entered the cab at the docks. He wanted to kick himself for not walking several blocks to cover their trail. He'd assumed Devil Town was still a free town, and that assumption had just put his daughter's life in danger.

He lay back on the chaise and gave Boden a quick look to see he hadn't moved. Reyne sighed. They were stuck in a basement in Devil Town where everyone—legal and illegal alike—had worked for the previous stationmaster. He suspected the same held true for the new stationmaster. For all he knew, Madame Grecklin was leading CUF to the basement at that exact moment.

CHAPTER 3

DROMADIER DILEMMA

Devil Town space docks, Spate
Throttle

THROTTLE SAW the squad of dromadiers the moment they entered the dock. Even though there were nearly a dozen other ships ahead of the *Gryphon* in line, she knew which ship they were headed for. She wheeled back to stay out of their view. She was only about halfway finished refueling, but she shut down the system without hesitation. The cables detached and retracted into the dock's fueling system.

She tapped a sequence of codes on her wrist comm, and a green light indicated she'd connected to the ship. Seconds later, two thin metal plates slid down the hull. The smaller one covered the ship's real registration number with a dummy number Demes had set up for her last year. She prayed the number still worked. The second, larger plate covered the teardrop painted on the hull. Since droms leaned toward a "shoot on sight" approach to any torrent they came across, she chose caution over chance.

After both panels clicked in place, she glanced under the ship to see the soldiers' legs. The squad was almost to the ship. Her breath caught. She sped up the ramp, placing herself in partial view, and boarded the *Gryphon*. The sound of running boot steps followed her until the door closed with its usual resounding boom of metal connecting with metal. She locked the hatch. Heart racing, she hurried to the bridge.

Behind her, a pounding on the door ensued. She could hear shouting, but the rilon hull muffled the voices too much to make out any words. Even so, she had no doubt they were ordering her to open up.

"No viggin' way I'm letting you onto my ship," she yelled back.

She didn't slow down as she reached the bridge, and plowed into her instrument panel hard enough to smash a kneecap. Good thing she couldn't feel anything from the waist down. She started to enter additional lockdown commands. Now that she was back on board, her mask fogged up, and she tore it off so she could see what she was doing.

A warning sounded, and the panel displayed the notification Throttle most certainly did *not* want to see:

Spate Dock Control initiating override control of your vessel per Collective Authority Code 468294. Prepare to be boarded.

Throttle flinched. "No."

She thought she'd have hours before the CUF initiated an override code, giving her time to come up with a plan. That they were already initiating the code meant they'd been onto the *Gryphon* the moment it hit orbit. No one had ever blocked the CUF override hack, not even Demes, which meant the *Gryphon* was about to be boarded and there wasn't a thing she could do to stop it. She entered a code on the panel and shoved away. Behind her, the wall opened to reveal a closet space barely wide enough for her wheelchair. She backed into the space and hit the only button on the wall. The door closed, leaving her in darkness.

Another warning sounded on the bridge, followed by the metallic sound of the ship's large door opening. The noise was soon followed by a stern male voice. "Your ship has been randomly selected for a dock check. Come out immediately, or you will be arrested."

Randomly selected, my ass. As the footsteps drew closer, she tried to calm her breathing. Light crept through around the edges, reminding her that even the smallest sound could be heard on the other side of the wall.

Reyne had built the space for her when she was seven years old. Back then, Reyne—her father not by blood but in all the ways that really mattered—drew plenty of attention of the unwanted kind from his involvement in the Fringe Uprising. His protectiveness drove her crazy, but she'd be damned if she didn't appreciate this tiny hideaway right now.

The sound of boot steps reached the bridge. Throttle's breath hitched, and she became a statue, even though every cell in her body thrummed with adrenaline. If they found her, they'd run her fake ID. Chances were, they'd also run a DNA scan, something far too expensive to fake. One scan, and she'd spend the rest of her life in a work camp, if she were lucky.

She'd had a few close calls with the CUF, but she'd never had to face them alone before. Adrenaline gave way to insecurity when she realized that, for the first time, there was no one there to help her. She was completely and utterly on her own.

She pursed her lips and girded her confidence. The hell she'd let insecurity get in her way.

The light around the door broke as someone walked far too close for her comfort. She held her breath until after the light returned, and until she heard the intruder tap on the ship's instrument panel. She cringed. No one had ever touched her panel before, and the action felt like a violation of her privacy.

While whoever was on the bridge pounded away on her

panel, the other droms conversed with one another as they searched the ship, but they were too far away for her to make out anything. No one yelled out again for her. After interminably long minutes, the bridge crasher quit hitting keys, and the bridge grew silent. Several minutes later, what sounded like a squad of boot steps walked off the ship, down the ramp, and left the *Gryphon* in silence.

Absolute silence.

Throttle's eyes widened. There was no constant hum of the ship's bio systems. No air circulation. The ship was perfectly sealed. Even without systems, she'd have breathable air for days. The problem was she'd never heard the ship door close behind the droms. Every bit of breathable air would be lost to the oxygen-depleted Spaten atmosphere.

She sucked in a breath. Another minute passed, and she found it harder to breathe. She wasn't claustrophobic, so she knew the urge to hyperventilate was coming from bad air.

In a rush, she thought through her only two options. She could close the door and restart the ship's systems, but then the droms would be back as soon as they heard the ship come back online. She decided to go with the second and only practical option. She'd grab her breather mask and hide until she was confident the squad had left the dock.

Vertigo spun her in the small space as she became more and more lightheaded. She realized then that she had a third option: die of asphyxiation.

She clenched her jaw as she reached up and hit the button. There was no viggin' way she'd die in a closet. The door opened, and she pushed herself forward to grab the breather.

Except it wasn't where she'd flung it.

Blackness tunneled her vision. In the center, she could see a masked drom leaning against her panel. He held out her breather. "Looking for this?"

She lunged for it.

He lifted the mask higher, just out of her reach.

She swung out to hit him. Her fist weighed a ton, and she fell from her chair. "Viggin' drom—" Her words slurred as she felt herself plummet into a cold black pit. She'd always figured she'd die at the hands of the CUF. She just didn't think it'd happen so soon.

CHAPTER 4

DEVIL TOWN BUSINESS

BODEN ROLLED over for the fourth time in as many minutes. Reyne knew the internal battle the recovering addict had been fighting while they hid in the drug den. The basement stunk of sweet soy, and Boden was clearly not as "recovered" as he'd been letting on the past few months.

They'd already been here too long—five hours and counting —but Madame Grecklin had locked the door at the top of the stairs, leaving them imprisoned in the dank room.

"How'd they know it was us?"

Reyne turned to see Boden watching him with bloodshot eyes.

Boden continued. "We were wearing breather masks. We used a fake account. I don't understand where we messed up."

Reyne shrugged. "I was telling Grecklin the truth. I don't think they have any idea who they're chasing. If they had any idea we were coming, there would've been ten times as many droms waiting to grab us the moment we stopped. My guess is they have orders to take in anyone who stops at Gin's."

Boden thought for a moment and seemed to accept Reyne's rationale, because he rolled over again. The thick haze in the room made Reyne groggy. He stood and paced to get his blood flowing.

After several minutes of pacing, he heard the door open, and Madame Grecklin emerged from upstairs. He turned back to Boden to see the man standing and alert.

"The streets cleared out about an hour ago," the woman said. "You should be okay to leave. But be careful. The windows have eyes around here."

Reyne nodded. "Thank you for your help, Madame."

She brushed him off, and then waved to a man who was slipping on a jacket. "Mr. Fitzroy."

"What?" the man asked before yawning.

"You're heading back to work at the docks, aren't you?"

He nodded. "Yeah, and I'm running late. You should've woken me thirty minutes ago."

She smiled. "My apologies. These two gentlemen could use a lift. I'm sure you wouldn't mind sharing company with two *generous* fellows."

Fitzroy's face perked up. "Generous, you say?"

"Mighty generous," Reyne added.

"Then, the more the merrier. I'm parked right outside." Fitzroy motioned to the stairs.

"Thank you, Madame," Reyne said. "We owe you."

She waved her hand in the air. "If your side turns out to be the winning side, keep me in mind. As a small business owner, life isn't grand. It's not easy making ends meet around here."

Reyne gave her a polite nod. The three men headed up the stairs. Reyne and Boden donned their breather masks before they entered the store, in case any customers were shopping. Fitzroy slid his mask on at the door, and they followed him outside to where a beater of a truck sat.

"Does it run?" Boden asked quietly behind Reyne.

Reyne was wondering the same thing, but he didn't say anything.

They all climbed in the front seat.

"The air system's busted, so you'll have to wear your masks," the man said as he started the vehicle. It came to life with a grumble and a lurch. Fitzroy went to shift it into gear, paused, and turned to Reyne. "I sure could use some good faith before we get on the road."

"Of course." Reyne fished out a large bill. "This should cover the energy cost to the docks."

The man's eyes grew wide. "Yeah. That'll do." He immediately shifted the truck into gear and headed down the road.

Fitzroy took them down several side roads, and they reached the docks faster than Reyne expected.

"Which dock do you need?" he asked.

"Hilo," Reyne said.

"Oh, the *private* docks. I should've known. Well, since you've been so nice and all, I'll give you a lift to your bay."

"Five," Reyne said, intentionally giving him the wrong number.

Fitzroy stopped at bay five, where a Myrad hauler sat, but Reyne was already looking down the line to where the *Gryphon* sat. His lips thinned, and his heart pounded. He shot Boden a quick glance, and by Boden's narrow gaze, it was clear he'd seen it already, too. A bright yellow Quarantine sign was posted by its ramp, and an entire squad of dromadiers stood on guard.

"You think Throttle's still on board?" Boden asked Reyne in a whisper.

"She has to be," Reyne answered.

"What's that?" Fitzroy asked.

Reyne didn't answer. As they climbed out of the truck, Fitzroy pointed at the *Gryphon*. "You're lucky your ship ain't the one down there. Looks like the CUF's laid claim to that one. Damn CUF buggers." He spat.

Reyne thought for a moment and then turned to Fitzroy. "How would you like to earn ten times what I paid you to drive us here?"

The man's jaw dropped. He clamped it back shut and tried to act casual, but was failing. "What do you have in mind?"

Spate, with little to offer in terms of resources, had become a melting pot of everything illegal in the Collective—drugs, gambling, prostitution. Every colonist in Devil Town had either participated in an illegal activity or at least touched dirty money. Reyne knew Fitzroy was a drug addict. He was hoping the man had other "flexible" scruples when it came to money.

"The CUF's claimed that ship, which means it doesn't belong to anybody in particular anymore, right?"

"Well, it belongs to the CUF buggers," Fitzroy countered.

Reyne nodded. "Agreed. But they have so many ships, they can't keep track of what they do and don't have."

Fitzroy kept watching him, like he didn't know where Reyne was going with this conversation.

"What if Dock Control received orders for that ship by ferry pilots bringing it to the armada? Then, there'd be no reason for the squad to remain here. Isn't that so?"

"Sure," he said. "But they don't have orders."

Reyne shrugged. "There's never been a mix-up around here?"

Fitzroy laughed. "There are mix-ups all the time. You've just got to grease the right wheels. Oh. *Oh.*" His eyes grew wide. He glanced at the Dock Control station for several long seconds, and then back at Reyne. "Thompson's working today. She can grant clearance, but she's not cheap. She just bought the newest Rosten last month. She's not a fan of the new stationmaster, so I think she'll do this."

Reyne fished out all his remaining credits and handed them to Fitzroy. "This should cover everything."

His eyes were as large as saucers. "It'll do." He pulled out a bill and tucked it into his pocket. "Give me a few minutes. I'll make it happen."

"No questions asked," Reyne cautioned.

"Shoot," he said. "I know better than to ask questions. I figure the less I know, the better off I am."

Fitzroy drove away. Reyne and Boden stepped under the hauler's shadow.

"You think he'll give the money to this Thompson and not drive off and keep it all for himself?"

Reyne sighed. "I sure hope so. This is how Devil Town operates. I'm counting on Fitzroy to have enough honor to keep his word."

Boden guffawed. "A drug addict?"

"You have honor," Reyne said, and Boden stiffened. He then added, "We'd best kept an eye out for trouble, just in case."

Boden unholstered a gun and held it behind him. Reyne followed suit.

At least fifteen minutes passed before Fitzroy returned in his truck. He stuck his head out the open window. "It's a go. You have ten minutes before they initiate launch. Oh, but she doesn't have a keycard to the ship. I'm afraid you're on your own for that."

"Leave that to me," Reyne said. "And the squad?"

Fitzroy pointed. "Looks like she's reporting the change in orders now."

They looked to see the squad checking their wrist comms. The dromadiers seemed pleasantly surprised that their guard duty was cancelled and wasted no time in departing. As soon as the squad disappeared around the corner, Reyne patted Fitzroy on the shoulder. "It was good doing business with you."

"Likewise," the man said. "Look me up the next time you're in Devil Town. I can help you find whatever you need."

"I'm sure you can," Reyne said, and he and Boden took off at a jog.

They ran up the ramp and on board the *Gryphon*. The door had been left open, and Reyne prayed Throttle had kept her breather mask on. He ran to the bridge and found the hidden closet door standing open and a breather mask on the floor. His heart dropped. "Throttle!" he yelled.

When she didn't respond, his heart began pounding. He pinged her wrist comm. "Search the ship!" he ordered Boden.

Boden ran through the ship, calling her name.

Reyne placed his hand on the instrument panel, and the ship systems came to life. He tried to focus on initiating launch prep sequences, but his mind kept going back to Throttle. If she wasn't on the ship, then where the hell was she?

Boden ran onto the bridge. "I can't find her anywhere," he said breathlessly. "What do we do now?"

Reyne grimaced. If they aborted the launch now, they'd never get another chance at getting the *Gryphon* back. But if Throttle was hiding somewhere in the docks...

His heart sank. His gut told him that if she wasn't on board, she wasn't in the docks. She hadn't responded to the ping, which meant something was preventing her from responding.

The droms had her.

Reyne exhaled slowly to suppress his terror. "Get back to the engines and prepare for jump speed."

"What? We can't leave Throttle behind."

"We have no idea where she is. They found the *Gryphon*, which means every drom on Spate will be searching for us. We can't do any good for Throttle if we get caught."

"We can't just give up on her."

"Trust me, I'm not giving up."

Boden clenched and unclenched his fists, glaring at Reyne. "What do we do now?"

"We head to the rendezvous point. Throttle would go there first. Now, buckle in and prep the engines for jump speed the instant we break out of atmo."

Boden stormed off the bridge.

Reyne opened the comm channel and immediately received contact.

"Phantom Five-One-Bravo, launch approved and sequenced. Launch upon your command."

Not even a countdown. This dock control was good. Reyne hit the comm. *"Dock Control, this is Phantom Five-One-Bravo. Launch acknowledged and approved. Thanks for your help."*

"Anytime. Watch out for patrols."

The *Gryphon* was launched by Dock Control from its bay and straight up into the atmosphere. Reyne fired the navigational engines, and the ship blasted through the sky at over ten Gs. When the ship broke through the last of Spate's atmosphere, he initiated jump speed.

With the system running the ship, Reyne pulled up an image of Spate. He gripped his armrests. He couldn't help but feel he'd left everything that mattered back in Devil Town.

CHAPTER 5

THE COASTAL RUN

The Space Coast
Heid

"BRING SHIELDS UP TO THIRTY PERCENT," Captain Gabriela Heid ordered.

She felt the crew's nervous glances being directed at her as they looked away from the screen filled with dots—each one representing a CUF drone—growing bigger every second.

When the distance hit three thousand, Heid said, "Enter stealth mode. Then, jettison the flak."

"Aye, aye, Captain," Sylvian replied.

A red border encircled the screen, the only on-ship visual sign that the *Arcadia* was in stealth mode. The warship was now effectively invisible to visual and radar systems alike.

Moments later, lights flickered against the blackness of space as chunks of garbage—each piece of flak repurposed with a small power generator—were ejected from the warship.

Heid had been in the CUF since she was fourteen, but her father had begun her teachings even earlier. She knew how the armada operated and knew how to exploit their dependency on automated defense systems. Drones were powerful tools with one critical weakness—they had no AI, therefore, no reasoning capability. Drones responded to threats exactly how they were programmed to. Heid had studied their programming, and knew things, like how drone sensors wouldn't pick up any traffic beyond a 2,800-click radius.

She also knew drones weren't equipped to scan for ships in stealth. Even so, Heid disliked using stealth. It burned juice at an exponential rate, and juice was at the top of their limited resources list. But even she acknowledged that stealth had its value, especially when she was planning to run a massive CUF blockade.

Her entire plan hinged on the assumption that drone programming hadn't been changed in over a year. It was a big assumption, since one of the armada's newest warships and a supply vessel now sat under torrent control.

Like clockwork, when the flak reached 2,800 clicks, the drones stationed at equal intervals across the entry to the Space Coast whirred to life and flashed red and white warning lights.

Heid continued to watch the distance close between them. At two thousand clicks, the drones fired at the flak. When no shots came at the *Arcadia,* Heid let out a breath. "Take us in, Will," she commanded.

"Taking us in," Will, the ship's pilot, said.

Before this moment, nothing larger than a Myrad cargo hauler had ever entered the Coast before. The *Arcadia,* a massive warship, was easily ten times the size of the Collective's largest hauler. Heid would've preferred to have taken a smaller ship in the specter fleet with stealth capability, but she needed the space for the refugees. At least, she hoped there were still refugees alive to rescue.

A rock hit the hull, sending a ripple through the ship.

"We're too big," Will said, a frantic tone to his words.

"You can do this, Will," she countered.

"I—I'll try," he stammered.

The Space Coast was an asteroid belt that sat outside the Collective's control. Up until a year ago, the CUF had ignored the Coast. Citizens avoided the Coast. Only the most adventurous colonists braved the asteroid belt to journey to the unauthorized colony situated in the middle of the Space Coast. Nova Colony sat inside a hollow asteroid that had been colonized by outlaws and smugglers as a sanctuary for those who needed to avoid the CUF. It had become the center of all less-than-legal business activities, and one of the few places offering colonists the opportunity to earn a decent living—or die trying.

A small asteroid hurtled at them. Will banked, but too late, and the rock the size of a house ricocheted off the bow. Two other asteroids followed in quick succession. Each hit made Heid cringe. As a rock scraped alongside the entire length of the hull, her hands gripped her armrest. "Will, don't break my ship."

"I'm trying. I mean, I'm trying *not to*," he stammered.

A massive asteroid filled the view screen.

Gasps and murmurs filled the bridge.

"I can't do this!" Will exclaimed.

Heid reached out to her panel. "Okay, Will. I'm taking the controls."

"Oh, thank the gods." Will's words drifted off as he slumped back from his panel.

No sooner did she take the controls, she leveled the ship, raised the bow slightly, then shoved the bow downward, arcing the massive warship under and around the asteroid in a half-loop. The *Arcadia* passed by the rock so closely she was surprised the asteroid didn't slice a hole across the hull.

She twisted the ship around the next asteroid and then the next, banking and corkscrewing through the Coast. If they'd been within a planet's atmosphere, the g-forces would've made nearly the entire crew either sick or pass out. But they'd been flying with minimal gravity, making the maneuvers feel more like a simulation than a real life-and-death race.

As they neared their destination at the Coast's center, the asteroids grew larger, but fewer, and Heid felt herself relax. When Nova Colony emerged onto the view screen, she smiled. "Hello, beautiful," she said softly to no one in particular. She maneuvered the *Arcadia* to lock on to the asteroid's outer rock. Once the locks clicked into place, she announced, "Sylvian, has one of the landers been loaded with standard emergency supplies?"

"Yes, Captain," Sylvian replied.

"Good. Prep all eight landers."

"Aye, aye, Captain."

Heid stood. "Will, the helm is yours."

"I have the helm." He turned around. "Captain, about what happened back there..."

Heid placed a hand on his shoulder "You did well. No ship this size is meant to fly through an asteroid belt. Trust me. With some practice in a patrol ship, you'll be able to handle the Coast in no time."

He sat a little straighter. "Thanks." Then he added, "I'll practice."

She smiled, left the bridge, and headed to landing bay One, where her lander sat.

Her gunman, Luther, stood waiting for her. Luther had joined her crew recently, after being freed from the Citadel back on Terra. She'd gained nearly twenty additional crewmembers from that batch. Many were in poor health, but all carried heavy vendettas in their hearts. Unlike her crew she'd had since serving the CUF, these new crewmembers often questioned her orders, and she worried she wouldn't be able to count on them if—*when*

—things went sour. They didn't trust her, which meant she couldn't trust them. Luther was the only one of her new members she somewhat trusted. Even then, she'd never want to put her life in his hands.

"From the sounds of things out there, I was beginning to wonder if you were trying to hit every asteroid in the Coast."

"Not *every* asteroid," she answered. "I wanted to save some for our flight out of here."

He gave a small nod that hinted he expected as much, and then led the way onto the lander. She buckled into the pilot's seat while Luther strapped in next to the door. Only two rode in each lander—the minimum required crew—to make room for as much cargo space as possible for transporting colonists back to the *Arcadia*.

Heid's lander departed the ship first, and the other landers followed hers into the large asteroid's jaw-like opening. She led them through a natural cave dimly lit by a single string of lights, and finally to the colony's docking station.

The docking station's doors stood open.

Heid opened a comm channel. "Nova Colony, this is specter flight of eight, requesting permission to dock."

No answer.

She repeated her request, and then tacked on, "Is anyone home?" When there was still no response, a rock settled in her gut. Were they too late? Had she waited too long to come?

"Don't worry," Luther said. "Colonists are tougher than you think. They're probably watching us right now, debating whether to drift us before or after they rob us."

"You think they'd shoot us when we dock?"

Luther shook his head. "Nah. They'd never do anything to hurt the ships. They're too valuable. These guys would wait until we all made it to the airlock and then suck out the air."

"That's not exactly reassuring."

"You want reassurance, see a therapist."

She pursed her lips and remained silent as she maneuvered the lander into docking position and slowly backed the small ship into a bay. Luther stood and extended the lander's braces. Locks clicked around the lander, securing it firmly in place.

"Well, if they want the landers, they've got them now," Luther said.

Her jaw tightened, and she stood. "Suit up and let's go."

The CUF had set up a drone blockade outside the Space Coast, closing off Nova Colony from the rest of the Collective. In the days that followed, many colonists had made a run for it. Most died, though a few had made it through the blockade without getting blown to pieces. Soon, there were no ships left in Nova Colony's docks, leaving all the remaining colonists stranded within the asteroid. Those colonists who'd remained had estimated they had a year left—if they were lucky—before they ran out of supplies, as no supply ships could reach them.

The blockade had been in place now for fourteen months.

The torrent captains had wanted to send ships earlier, but their hands had been tied. The CUF had implemented martial law across the entire fringe, and it was getting near-impossible for torrent ships to travel through the system without running across a CUF ship or drone of some kind. It had taken the *Arcadia* two months of zigging and zagging across the fringe to make it to the Space Coast. Even with taking an obscure route, the torrent warship had had to enter stealth mode three times on their way to the Coast, burning nearly half their juice. They'd use up most of it by the time they left the Coast, leaving no room to evade or fight off any unwanted company they might run into on their return trip.

The seven other landers positioned into docks as Heid and Luther exited their craft and hooked their suits onto the zip lines rigged into the bedrock. With no gravity in the docks, Heid shot small bursts from her suit's propulsion system to shoot across the dock to the other side, where the airlock stood open. Luther came up right behind her.

They disconnected their suits from the zip line and propelled through the doorway. Heid flew over to the airlock's far side, where a screen and a large button were encased in the metal wall. She tapped the button, and the airlock door closed behind them. Air shot out from nozzles in the walls, obscuring the tiny enclosure in a cloud. Artificial gravity came without warning, and they landed on the ground with jarring *thuds*. As they climbed to their feet, the moisture cloud dissipated, and the monitor on the wall lit up in green.

Heid double-checked the air level on her wrist comm. Safe, but marginally so. Guilt sat like a heavy stone in Heid's gut. Tainted air was a common problem in ships and on space stations if the air filters failed. At this level, it would've taken only weeks before bronchial infections set in. She swallowed, hoping the air levels dropped only recently. If they were too late, it would be on her.

She tapped her wrist comm. "Heid to *Arcadia*."

"*Arcadia here, Commander.*"

"Notify Jovovich to prep an air filter kit."

"*Copy that, Commander.*"

She removed her helmet, inhaled cold air, and coughed. The air had a foul flavor, like she'd been stuck in an elevator crammed with people. Her next breath was smaller. Luther removed his helmet soon after.

The door leading to the interior opened, and the pair found themselves facing a dozen gaunt-faced colonists. Heid would've felt relief at seeing the colonists alive except that every single one of them was pointing a rifle in her and Luther's direction.

She spoke, careful not to make any movement. "I'm Captain

Heid of the *Arcadia,* and this is Luther Jackson of Terra. We're here to rescue you."

A stocky man in the group's center looked at Luther, then turned his gaze onto Heid. He looked her up and down slowly. His eyes narrowed. "You'd better convince us right quick that you're not CUF, or else you're going to be taking a swim out on the Coast in three seconds."

A couple members of the group coughed in between ragged breaths.

Heid held one hand out as she reached toward her suit ever so slowly.

"Watch yourself," the man cautioned.

She paused. "I can convince you if you give me one moment of latitude."

The seconds dragged on long, until he gave the smallest nod.

Heid reached into a pocket on her suit, and pulled out the teardrop-shaped pendant—the emblem of the torrents—and held it high for them to see. She tucked the pendant back into her suit. "I'm not CUF, and the longer you stand around with your heads up your asses, the greater chance the CUF is going to get suspicious about why so much space junk showed up all of sudden around their drone blockade."

The man's lips thinned. "I didn't believe the stories. I thought they were too farfetched. I'd never heard of a CUF commander changing sides before, let alone taking a warship with her."

"It's your lucky day," she said. "You can fly on that warship if you so choose."

After a moment, he glanced back to the people with him. "Put down your weapons."

They nearly dropped their weapons as they slumped and coughed. A few leaned against the wall.

The man held out his hand to Heid. "I'm Stan. Operations Manager of Nova Colony."

Heid shook it. "Time is not on our side. The *Arcadia* is waiting to give anyone a lift to Playa, where we have living quarters set up for everyone."

"How can it be any safer than here?" Stan asked. "The last news we saw, the CUF has put the entire fringe under martial law."

"They have," Heid said. "But, since they bombed Ice Port, they have written Playa off. They assume no one can land or take off on Playa." Her lips curled upward. "They have no idea we have an operational space dock."

Stan eyed her for a moment before shaking Luther's hand. "So, it's true?" Stan asked. "There's a new torrent Uprising?"

Luther answered. "It's called the Fringe Liberation Campaign, my friend, and it's shaping up to be far bigger than the first Uprising. We've even managed to snag a CUF supply ship of our own."

"We'll fill you in on the way," Heid cut in. "The CUF will have sent in patrol ships to inspect the blockade. We don't have time to delay. How many colonists are in Nova Colony?"

Stan grimaced. "Two hundred and eighty-four."

"Eighty-three," a man behind Stan corrected. "We lost Jadin yesterday."

Heid's heart sank. Based on all her calculations, the number should've been higher.

"What happened?" Luther asked.

Stan shrugged. "We'd already been on tight rations before the air filters started to fail. When the lung infections hit, we didn't have near enough antibiotics. There wasn't anything we could do."

"Damn, that's rough," Luther said.

Guilt nagged at Heid. After all, it was she who'd stolen the warship and launched the Fringe Liberation Campaign. She knew the blame sat squarely on her shoulders for every death at

Nova Colony. She'd wanted to come sooner, but it'd taken too long to build the generators for the flak, and her Spate mission had consumed far more of her time than she'd planned. But she'd chosen Spate over Nova Colony—she'd have to live with the consequences.

Heid tapped her comm. "All lander crews are authorized to enter the colony to assist with evacuation." She turned back to Stan. "There's room for everyone on the landers. Make an announcement to evacuate. We'll assist anyone too weak to walk."

"I'm not leaving," Stan said. "This rock might not be pretty, but she's my responsibility. I'm not leaving her. And I know a few others will stay. Some folks have never been off this rock and don't intend to leave it now."

Heid watched him for a moment. "I expected as much, and I have a lander full of supplies that should cover your needs for a while. But I can give no guarantees how soon we'll be out here again. You could be on your own for some time."

"I can live with that," Stan said, and he turned to the people behind him. "Go on and get your groups packed up. Move the weakest first. Make sure anyone who doesn't want left behind isn't left behind."

Too many hours later, the *Arcadia* departed Nova Colony with two hundred and forty-five additional passengers. The sickest had been sent immediately to Medical, while several of the strongest had refused to let Heid leave their sight.

As they stood on the bridge, they eyed Heid and her crew with trepidation and sideways glances. She knew what was going through their heads. They were on a CUF ship, and though Heid and her crew no longer wore uniforms, they carried on flying the *Arcadia* with many of the same military processes and procedures they'd used while still in the CUF.

To these new colonists, Heid and her crew had ties with their enemy. They'd boarded her ship out of desperation rather than trust, not that she'd expected them to trust her. Not that she trusted them—she didn't trust anyone who was desperate. She tapped a message to her bridge crew and security teams.

REMAIN ON HIGH ALERT. REPORT ANY ISSUES IMMEDIATELY.

The new colonists were sick and weak, but they were also survivors. She knew a wounded coyote could be most dangerous when trapped.

An idea formed in her mind.

She took the controls and looked out across the Coast, out beyond, to where she knew the drones and likely several CUF patrol ships stood. She stated her order loudly and clearly. "Arm all photon guns, and fire up phase cannons one through five. We're going to blast every drone out of the sky."

Her crew turned to her, eyes wide. The new passengers eyed her with surprise—hope, even.

Will spoke first. "The CUF will know we were here."

Her navigator added, "They'll know we've evacuated the Coast."

"Oh, they won't have any reason to blockade a colony they believe is abandoned," Sylvian said.

"Exactly." Heid's lips curled into a smile. "Now, let's have some fun."

CHAPTER 6

ACHES AND PAINS AND DOPPELGANGERS

Devil Town fringe station, Spate
Throttle

THROTTLE WOKE in a bed instead of on a hard, cold prison floor. She hadn't expected to wake at all.

Her pounding head assured her she was alive. She lifted her head and immediately lowered it back to the pillow. The room swirled around her, and her tongue felt thick. Whatever they'd drugged her with was still deep in her system. Her mind was too fuzzy to process any logic behind drugging a prisoner—a paraplegic one at that. The CUF used stun guns, which were cheaper and easier to use than drugs, and droms tended to enjoy using pain-inflecting weapons more often.

She glanced at her forearm to find her wrist comm missing. It was then she noticed she was wearing a hospital gown rather than her clothes.

She pushed herself into a sitting position, and the room spun so quickly she became nauseous. She reached out for her wheelchair, but it wasn't where she always left it. Her head swayed as she searched the room, squinting through her double vision. Her chair was missing. Anxiety began to clear her sight. Without her chair, the droms didn't need to put her in a prison cell. It wasn't like she could haul herself out of there—wherever *there* even was—without drawing the attention of any drom in the area. Her only chance was if they passed out from laughing so hard at the sight of a crippled girl dragging herself around Spate.

Shoot, she would've laughed at the idea if she could've seen straight.

A lock clicked, and Throttle turned to see the door slide open and two men and two women walk in. Two pairs of twins. No, that wasn't right. She blinked and tried to focus her vision. One man, and one woman a step behind him. He was tall for a Myrad, with the bluest skin she'd ever seen. His family must've been one of the first colonists on Myr, or he'd had his skin stained. With the vibrant colors he wore and the way he carried himself, she suspected it was the former.

The woman, on the other hand, had pale white skin—maybe even a shade paler than Throttle's—with green eyes and dark auburn hair. She was stunningly beautiful and wore a long green gown. She was also incredibly familiar, yet Throttle was sure she'd never seen the woman before in her life.

Throttle rested her head against the wall to help hold it steady.

"The drugs will wear off soon," The man said. "But I wanted to see you as soon as you woke."

Throttle tried to focus on him. "Why am I still alive?"

He watched her. "You're Halit Herley, pilot and mail runner. You earned the nickname of Throttle due to your reputation for flying fast. Tell me, Ms. Herley, why didn't you take your adoptive father's surname? For all intents and purposes, you're Halit Reyne. There's no way you could remember your real parents."

She gritted her teeth and repeated, "Why am I still alive?"

He smiled, an expression devoid of humor and full of arrogance. "I suppose I should introduce myself. I'm Axos Wintsel, the stationmaster of Devil Town." He motioned to the woman standing behind him, who never looked up. "And this is my consort, Qelle."

Ah. That's why the woman looked familiar. The fog was slowly clearing from Throttle's mind, but everything still felt sluggish, like she was stuck in a tank of pudding.

"You and I have something in common," he said, with a sly smile on his face.

"A colonist and a Myrad have something in common?" She belted out a dry laugh. "Let me guess. You're a cripple, too."

"I am not a cripple!" He stomped toward her with a raised fist.

She braced herself for the blow.

He took a deep breath, lowered his hand, and took a step back. "No, I am not a cripple. We're orphans, you and me. For each of us, our only family left is our adoptive fathers, which makes me feel like we're kindred spirits. Your parents were killed in the Uprising, as was my father. I lost my mother far more recently. Perhaps you've heard of her. Her name was Dr. Zara Wintsel."

Throttle's lips parted, and she quickly erased all expression from her face in an attempt to hide her knowledge, though she suspected she wasn't doing a very good job at it through the drug-induced haze. "Don't know her."

He looked disappointed. "I think you do. After all, it was Aramis Reyne who killed her." He moved closer.

Throttle tried not to cringe.

He continued. "Don't worry. I don't believe in punishing the child for the sins of her father."

"Somehow, I find that hard to believe," she said.

"It's true. I'll even prove it," he said, and the slinky smile returned. Throttle would've sprinted from the room that exact moment if she could have.

"Qelle." He held out his hand.

The woman approached, and placed an electronic device on his palm before taking a step back in a subservient pose. He looked at the device for a brief moment before turning back to Throttle.

"How long do you think you were out?" he asked.

She shrugged. "A couple hours."

He chuckled. "Not quite. You were unconscious for over two days."

Two days. Chills climbed through her. Reyne and Boden would be so worried about her. Chills became ice. If they hadn't tried to rescue her by now, that meant they thought she was dead. Worse, they were dead. A weight settled on her chest, and breathing became a labor.

"You're not curious as to why you were unconscious for so long?"

Throttle forced a deadpan expression. "You get your rocks off watching women sleep?"

He ignored her. "How about I show you?" He held up the device, and pressed his thumb on its small screen.

Sensation stormed through her legs, and she grabbed them. She felt the warm pressure of her hands on her legs—not just through her hands, but also through her legs. Goosebumps swam all the way down her body, and her legs tingled. She ran her hands across her thighs, noticing the touches felt real and not like phantoms.

Her foot spasmed, and her leg moved. Her leg had moved! Tears welled in her eyes, blurring her vision, and she hastily wiped them away to keep watching her legs. She willed her feet to lift, and they did, though the motion felt foreign.

"The surgery didn't take long," he said. "Much of the time

was spent rebuilding and strengthening the atrophied muscles in your legs. Go ahead. Try to stand."

Throttle swallowed, and swung her legs over the side of the bed. She'd spent her entire life dreaming of this moment. Of being able to stand on her own without the help of any wheelchair or braces. Every night, she dreamed of walking onto the *Gryphon's* bridge while Reyne watched her, smiling.

Unlike her dream, a stranger stood smiling at her. Not just any stranger. Her enemy.

She didn't push off the bed. Instead, she remained sitting. It was the hardest thing she'd ever done in her life. She craved to stand more than anything, to run and jump and hop. But she didn't move.

She took a breath and then looked up at Axos. "Why?"

He cocked his head. "Because I'm hoping we can be friends."

"That's a load of bull," she snapped. "What game are you playing?"

"No game."

The way he pursed his lips in humor said the opposite.

"So, I can just stand and walk out of here," she said.

"If you'd like. However, I should caution you that you want me as a friend, not an enemy." He held up the device and pressed the button.

Fire burned down Throttle's spine and through her legs. She cried out and clutched her quadriceps. Then, as suddenly as the agony had hit her, it disappeared, leaving a numbing coldness in its wake. She sucked in a breath and squeezed her knees. She felt nothing.

She glared at Axos. "What did you do?"

He wagged the device at her. "See this little thing? It controls the implant in your spine. I can turn the implant on or off with a simple swipe of my thumbprint. I don't want to hurt you, but you forced my hand when you were unruly."

She clenched her teeth. "What do you want from me?"

His lips curled upward. "Now, I think we're getting somewhere." He pulled up a chair. The woman behind him didn't move, keeping her gaze directed at the floor.

"My adoptive father, I'm sure you know, is none other than Corps General Michel Ausyar. He asked me to fill the position as stationmaster of Devil Town." He waved his hand. "Now, it's not a glamorous job, but it's temporary, and a means to an end. Once all the space docks are under Ausyar's command, I'll no longer need to waste time here in the fringe and can move on to something far more fitting of my heritage."

Throttle bit her tongue to keep from making a crude remark about exactly what she thought of his heritage.

"That's where you can help me," he said.

She frowned. "How so?"

"This Fringe Liberation Campaign is causing delays in our plans. The sooner we can put that little rebellion behind us, the sooner I can return to Myr and you can live a life as a complete person, no longer a crippled colonist. All you have to do is help me find Aramis Reyne."

He's still alive!

Relief relaxed her taut muscles, though only slightly. She now understood the reason she was still alive. Axos expected her to be a traitor, bait, or both. She nearly rolled her eyes. "You want me to lead you to Reyne so you can kill him."

Axos held up a hand. "Oh, by the eversea, no. I need Reyne alive. Ausyar wants a public execution. It will help draw out the remaining torrent leaders."

His wrist comm chimed. He read a message, sighed, and stood. "Pressing business has arisen. I must be on my way. We'll continue our conversation later." He smoothed his clothes and turned to leave. He paused. "Qelle will fetch your meal, as I imagine you're famished." With that, he left without another word.

Qelle followed him out, and the door closed and locked behind them.

Throttle was left alone. She rubbed her legs, but they felt no different than they'd felt for the past twenty years. *Dead weight.*

She could have her legs back. All she had to do was sell her soul to a blue-skinned devil.

She exhaled and fell back onto the pillow. She was never one to feel sorry for herself, and she wasn't going to start now. Instead, she needed to do something productive, like figure out a way out of here. She was fairly sure she was at the stationhouse, which meant she was a long way from the docks. The room itself didn't seem too secure. A simple lock on the door would be easy enough to bypass. As for the camera...

She'd known she was being watched by the Myrad's conveniently-timed arrival within minutes of her waking, and she could guarantee a drom was watching her now.

Throttle looked around. *There you are.* In the corner, near the door, a small camera hung from the ceiling. The room was small, and a single camera easily covered the entire space. Still, she searched for other cameras, but found none. She winked at the camera.

The camera was a simple black orb, which meant it wasn't infrared. She assumed all the cameras in the station were the same. *Good.* If she moved only in darkness, she'd avoid detection —not that she had any idea how to cut power to the room and hallways from where she sat.

Now, the biggest hurdle. Her legs. Even if she could get out of the room undetected, without a wheelchair and a breather mask, any full escape attempt was doomed.

She sighed and leaned back. Without a ship, she was helpless.

The door clicked and whooshed open. In walked Qelle with a tray of food.

The woman eyed Throttle tentatively, and then stepped inside. "I brought you food." She set the tray on Throttle's lap and took a quick step back.

"It's okay. I don't bite," Throttle said.

"Axos cautioned me that you may be unpredictable," she said without making eye contact.

"Qelle, I'm *paralyzed.* How unpredictable do you think I can be?"

She shrugged.

Throttle turned her attention to the tray with a bowl of black philoseed hash and a glass of an electrolyte drink. Axos had been right about one thing. She was hungry. She ate a spoonful of hash and took another. In between bites, she said, "So, Axos can't swing any decent grub around here?"

Qelle flustered. "I'm sorry. Everyone except Axos and his leadership team eat hash at every meal. It's what I eat as well. With the space dock on Darios still out of commission—"

"Don't worry about it," Throttle interrupted. She watched the woman for a lengthy moment. Qelle was nothing how Sixx described. Sure, she was beautiful, but Sixx talked about her spirit and strength. This woman seemed devoid of both.

Throttle ate the rest of her meal in silence. After taking a long drink, she spoke again. "You're even prettier than your picture."

Qelle frowned and looked up for the first time. "My picture?"

"Yeah, Sixx has one in his cabin. He's never stopped looking for you, you know."

"Sixx?" Her confused look morphed into one of understanding. "Oh, I'm not Qelle Sixx."

Throttle lowered her glass. "If you're not Jeyde Sixx's wife, then who are you?"

"I'm not her. I mean, I'm Qelle, but not really."

"So, you're not Qelle Sixx of Spate."

The woman shook her head. "No. I'm from Darios."

Throttle cocked her head. "But you look just like her. Your name's Qelle."

"I'm not her." She began to speak faster and softer. "He liked her face, but he didn't like her personality. She made him angry, and he killed her."

"Oh." Throttle frowned. Sixx wouldn't be happy to hear that.

Qelle continued. "Axos designed Qelle's face on another servant who was more obedient."

"You," Throttle said.

She shook her head. "I'm Qelle Delta. There were three Qelles before me."

"Let me guess," Throttle said. "They also made him angry."

Qelle swallowed and then nodded. "He has a bit of a temper."

"You're telling me." She took a drink. This woman was scared of her own shadow and would be of no help to Throttle in escaping.

The woman's wrist comm chimed, and she jumped. "I have to go. Lily is looking for me."

"Who's Lily?" Throttle asked.

Qelle's eyes went wide. "Oh, I shouldn't have said that." Her gaze shot frantically to the door before turning back to Throttle. "She's Axos's daughter."

"Ah," Throttle said. "And let me guess. Her mother was Qelle Sixx."

Qelle Delta nodded.

Throttle's gaze narrowed. "Does Lily know the truth?"

She shook her head in a rush. "And she can't. Axos would be furious. He wants her to grow up with both parents."

"Even if one's a fake."

"I'd better go." The woman picked up the tray and hustled to the door. She opened it to reveal a young girl of maybe seven or eight standing there. The girl had auburn hair, green eyes, and the slightest blue hue to her skin.

"What are you doing here, dear? You should be studying."

"I'm done, Qelle." The girl then peeked around the woman to make eye contact with Throttle.

Throttle immediately knew who she was. "Hi, Lily."

The girl gave a quick glance at Qelle before looking at Throttle again. Then the door closed, cutting them off.

Throttle stared at the door for a long time. She couldn't make out what the girl was thinking, but there was sharp intelligence in those eyes. She hadn't said much, but what she'd said told Throttle everything she needed to know.

Lily had called the woman Qelle, not Mother. She *knew*.

Throttle felt hope rise within her, and a plan formed in her mind. Maybe, just maybe, a little girl could help Throttle escape.

CHAPTER 7

A NEW PLAN

Tulan Canyon, Playa
Heid

HEID PLOPPED down on the chair in front of Vym's desk. "Only eighty-two Nova colonists have joined my crew. The rest show no interest whatsoever in joining the fight."

"Do you blame them?" Vym glanced up from the computer screen in her desk. "They've faced death and survived. They deserve to enjoy a normal life. We can't force them to fight. We made it clear: every torrent is a volunteer."

"I know," Heid said with a sigh. "It's just that the CUF outnumbers us ten to one."

"A hundred more would make little difference. In fact, a hundred more could hurt us if their hearts weren't into the Campaign. The difference will come from the grassroots torrents who stand for their rights in each of the colonies. That's who will win the Campaign." The old woman pursed her lips. "News of your trip to Nova Colony has already made the headlines."

Heid tried to suppress a grin, but failed. "I saw them."

Vym raised her brows. "Did you really have to destroy every single CUF drone you came across?"

Heid held up her hand. "I didn't destroy the drones. The Nova colonists pulled the triggers." Her smile grew wider. "But it was rather fun."

"Your fun escalated the Campaign. From what I hear, the CUF is cracking down harder on every colony now. We've recalled the specters from Darios and Spate."

The younger woman waved her off. "The CUF is looking for *any* excuse to bring down more pressure."

Vym wagged her finger in a motherly scold. "You and Critch both excel at giving them excuses. I hear Parliament hired private firms to rebuild the Ice Port space docks. Evidently, they're feeling the loss of rilon production in their pocketbooks."

Heid's eyes widened. "What if they discover Tulan Base? This dock isn't that far from Ice Port."

Vym's gaze narrowed. "Believe me, I'm not letting any citizen get their grubby hands on Ice Port. I lost Ice Port once. Never again. Those private firms are going to discover Playa is becoming a well-armed planet with drones of its own."

Heid straightened, a look of shock crossing her face. "You've been building drones? When are you launching them?"

"They're already in orbit. Your scanners didn't pick them up because they're made out of pure rilon, and their electronics are shielded. I learned a thing or two from my time as a stationmaster."

Heid laid a hand on the desk. "Incredible." She eyed Vym. "The moment the first shot is fired, the CUF will know our base is here. They'll bring the entire armada here."

Vym's door chimed and Jed Baptiste entered. He strode over, smiled warmly, and clasped Heid's hand in both of his hands. "Gabriela, it's been too long."

"You look great," Heid said. The older man walked with a

limp from his time spent as a prisoner in the Citadel. If he didn't have the limp, Heid could've sworn she was looking at new man. He'd put on at least thirty pounds, and had shaved his beard. At his age, she'd never expected him to recover from imprisonment. She'd also had the same thought about Vym, who'd proven her just as wrong.

"Your timing is perfect, dear," Vym said. "We were just going to talk about Terra."

Jed leaned against Vym's desk. "Excellent. Don't stop on my account."

Dear? Heid had known that Vym and Jed spent quite a bit of time together, but she'd assumed their time was spent in managing all the printing operations and refugee camp. As she saw the pair together now, the attraction was obvious, and Heid smiled. Clearly, the old CUF commandant and the Ice Port stationmaster had found time for themselves as well.

"We need to make sure the CUF is stopped at Terra," Vym said, bluntly cutting into Heid's thoughts. "Gabriela, I need you to travel to Terra. That's where we'll make our stand."

Startled, Heid looked from Vym to Jed. "Every CUF ship in the armada has orders to attack the *Arcadia* on sight. If I fly the warship in front of the armada, I'm flaunting that I stole a ship. Even when the Fringe Liberation Campaign is over, they'll still go after the *Arcadia* with everything they've got. It's a matter of pride for them. Flying in front of the armada will get me shot. How will that help the Campaign?"

Vym raised a finger. "Terra is a tense situation, but every day we're reclaiming another block or two of Rebus Station. Soon, we'll reach the docks. I suspect that Ausyar will not take defeat quietly."

"Our fleet is no match against the armada in a large-scale battle, but you can take on a single warship," Jed said. "The *Arcadia* is our ace in the hole. With the modifications we've made to it, your ship can take Ausyar's *Unity* in a fair fight. We've leaked intel that we plan to attack the citizen planets, which means the other three warships will remain at Alluvia and Myr. If you can reach Terra by the time we take the docks, you can ensure that victory on Terran soil can be matched by a victory in Terran space."

Vym nodded. "With the Myrad recession looming closer to a depression, citizens have little appetite for an expensive war. If we take Terra, Parliament will be forced to consider a peace treaty."

Jed spoke. "Critch has informed me that the *Unity* is the only warship that remains in Terran orbit, but it has frigates and destroyers defending it as well. We can't risk the *Arcadia* against a full complement."

"It can win," Heid countered.

Vym pursed her lips. "The odds aren't in your favor."

"The specters are on their way to Terra, but you will reach Terra first," Jed said. "While we need to take Rebus Station, we hope to have our fleet there when it happens. We can't afford losing this fight."

Heid sat straighter. "I can promise you that I'll do everything in my power to put an end to Ausyar's games."

"I know, but be careful, Gabriela," Vym cautioned. "If you're spotted, Ausyar may have time to call reinforcements. If we lose the *Arcadia*, we lose everything."

"Don't worry," Heid said. "I'll keep the *Arcadia* a couple quadrants out from Terran airspace. Ausyar's radar will never pick us up."

Jed gave a wistful smile. "If I wasn't so old, I'd be up there with you in a ship of my own."

Vym patted his hand. "Oh, Jed. You're not too old." She turned to Heid. "He's staying here to manage munitions production. I can't manage printing operations and play mother to the two hundred and forty-one additional souls you brought to Tulan Base."

Heid smirked, imagining hard-nosed Vym as a mother.

The older woman continued. "Later today, I plan to announce a rationing plan. How well do you think that will go over, considering these people nearly starved to death a month ago? Without Darios, I need a miracle to find an additional food supply line to Playa. I'm even considering using the *Matador* as a food supply ship."

"About the *Matador*..." Heid began. "Using it for food helps in the short-term, but I have an idea I'd like to discuss with you that may help with the growing number of refugees in the long-term. Remember the original generation ships that brought settlers to Alluvia?"

Vym's lips thinned. "I'm not sure I like where you're going with this."

Jed narrowed his gaze. "Hear her out."

Heid continued. "I've already worked out the details. If we—"

Vym held up her hand, cutting Heid off. Something on her computer panel had drawn her attention, and she didn't look up from it. "I believe Seda just surpassed Critch and you for talent in causing trouble. This hit the networks three hours ago." She transferred her panel's display to the wall display. Seda Faulk, the Rebus Station stationmaster, faced the camera. He wore a short-sleeved shirt, putting his artificial arm on display, no doubt to add to the effect.

This is Stationmaster Seda Faulk with a message to all people, citizens and colonists alike. One year ago, martial law was illegally enacted across the entire Collective by Corps General Ausyar of the Collective

Unified Forces Armada in response to my discovery and release of wartime prisoners who'd not been released at the end of the Fringe Uprising of 2910. Holding prisoners after a war has ended is in direct conflict with Collective Rule Fourteen A. Yet, these prisoners, which included both citizens and colonists, were held, against their will, for over twenty years. The Collective has made no move to compensate these innocents for their loss.

Parliament has made multiple attempts to bury this truth. That Parliament no longer strives to uphold the Collective Rules means Parliament no longer represents the needs of the people. I have previously declared independence for Terra. I now represent all colonies. As of this date, November Fourteen, 3014, all colonies declare full independence from the Collective. Each colony will stand on its own, governing itself and establishing its own laws. Stationmasters will be selected by colonists. No colonists will participate in the false Parliament. If colonies wish to trade with other colonies or with Alluvia or Myr, trade agreements may be formed.

As of this moment, the Collective, including the Collective Unified Forces, has no authority over any colony. The colonies are now independent, free from taxation and military oppression. Should CUF forces attempt to exert force or control over any colony, all colonists have full rights and responsibilities to stand against their illegal invaders.

This declaration has been approved by representatives of each colony, including Terra, Darios, Spate, Playa, and Nova Colony. We do not speak for Alluvia and Myr. Attached to this broadcast is a copy of the colonies' decla-

ration of independence in all languages and all file formats.

The broadcast ended with a brief image of the torrent teardrop, followed by a display of all five colony flags.

"I'm surprised his broadcast hasn't been pulled yet," Jed said. "He must have a talented hacker to get that speech across all the networks."

"He does," Heid said. "Demes connected us. Her name's Vapor. She's done one or two projects for me."

"As you can see, you need to get to Terra," Vym said. "The colonies have just declared war against the Collective."

"I'll have the *Arcadia* loaded with the full nine yards," Heid said as she pushed to her feet. She started to head to the door, then paused. "By the way, who was the Playa representative who signed the declaration of independence?"

Vym smiled. "Yours truly. I told you, I have no intention of ever losing my colony again."

CHAPTER 8

DIFFERENT DIRECTIONS

Tulan Canyon, Playa
Reyne

REYNE AND BODEN arrived at rendezvous point Alpha, and Throttle was nowhere to be seen. When they landed, Reyne strode into Vym Patel's office. "Have you seen Throttle?"

The old woman frowned. "Why would I have seen Throttle? She went with you to Spate."

Reyne collapsed in a chair. "She stayed with the ship when Boden and I went to meet Gin James. She was missing when we returned, and the CUF had a squad posted at the ship."

Vym leaned forward. "Then we must assume she's either a prisoner or dead. And if she's a prisoner, she won't be alive for long."

Reyne's lips thinned. "I need to find her."

"I'll put ears out around Devil Town, but it's become more difficult to get information with martial law everywhere. Tell me your meeting with Gin went well, at least."

"It never happened." Reyne waved his hands. "Gin was executed by the new stationmaster."

"There's a new stationmaster?" Vym's brows lifted in surprise. "Parliament has never moved so fast before."

"It's Axos Wintsel," Reyne said.

"A Myrad?" Vym filled two glasses with liquor as she thought. "Why, he can't be older than twenty-five, thirty at most. He's far too young to be a stationmaster. What could Mason possibly achieve with a Myrad as a stationmaster?"

She handed him a glass, and he took a drink before speaking. "We haven't heard a peep from Mason in over a year. Who's to say he's still pulling the Collective's strings? Maybe he was ousted from power."

"Mason—Gabriel Heid—is not someone you simply *oust* from power. The only way to accomplish that would be to kill him, and his death would splash across all the headlines. It's when he's gone quiet that I begin to worry the most. With nearly half the Founders missing, disavowed, or broken off from his control, I imagine he's grown quite desperate to see his ideology made a reality."

Reyne shook his head. "Mason's ideology is insanity."

"Is it?" Vym countered. "We all want a unified Collective."

"His unified Collective would be under a despot's rule. We want equality, not slavery."

"But we all desire peace. He's always seen himself as working for the greater good. He firmly believes that."

"He still deserves to die for the thousands he's killed."

"I absolutely agree with you," she said, downing the remainder of her drink. "And I hope to see the look on his face before I send him into the abyss."

Reyne finished off his drink. "I'd like to make that happen." He set down the empty glass and looked out the window. "It looks like Tulan Base is growing. How's production?"

"We're running at optimum production levels. It took over a month to print a second 3D printer using the first, but once that was built, we had one printer for printing munitions and supplies, and a second printer producing more printers. We're now at twelve printers operating thirty hours a day, seven days a week."

His brows rose. "That puts us well ahead of schedule. How are you managing to find enough labor for packaging and loading?"

"Heid brought over two hundred Nova colonists back with her. Over one hundred of them are helping out around here. Another eighty joined her crew, and the remainder are still recovering from their time on Nova Colony." Then Vym smiled. "It seems Gabriela made quite a statement on the return trip. Evidently, there wasn't a single drone left by the time she was finished. The colonists are quite taken with her."

Reyne chuckled. "I bet that caught her father's notice. Where's she? I need to catch up with her."

"She's on her way to Terra."

"Terra? Why's she going there? It's too risky. Ausyar has an entire armada in orbit over Rebus Station."

Vym held up her hands. "She and a few Nova colonists worked out a plan. It's better if she tells you it herself."

Reyne frowned. "I can't go to Terra. I need to stay here in case—when—Throttle arrives."

"Haven't you heard?" Vym asked.

"Heard what?"

"Seda Faulk declared independence for the fringe. He stated every colony has the right to govern itself." She inhaled deeply. "It made quite the headlines."

"I can imagine. If Seda didn't have a bulls-eye on his back before, he sure has one now. I take it he and Sixx made it back to Terra?"

She nodded. "Yes, but I didn't receive any update on how their trip to Myr went." She tapped a finger on the table. "You're doing Throttle and the Fringe Liberation Campaign no good here. The Campaign has escalated, and Rebus Station has become a warfront. The *Arcadia* is loaded with everything we've got, but Heid is still young. And Critch can be rash—he needs you there to balance him. The Campaign needs you there. There's nothing you can do for Throttle from here, Aramis. I promise, I'll send in people I can trust to Spate to find out what happened. I'll send word the moment I hear something."

He thought for a long, agonizing moment before abruptly pushing to his feet. "Okay, then. I guess I'm off to Terra. It's only Boden and me on the *Gryphon* right now, so if you happen to have any torrents ready to go fight, I can take a dozen."

"I'll have a dozen eager torrents on your ship within the hour."

He strode from Vym's office without so much as a goodbye. Once he left, his pace slowed before he stopped. He braced against the wall to keep from collapsing. Tears welled in his eyes, and he clenched his fists.

He'd convinced himself Throttle had somehow avoided the CUF and would be here waiting for him. That she wasn't here meant the CUF had her. He knew the odds of ever seeing her alive again were infinitesimally small, but he refused to give up.

He had to head to Terra, but as soon as he was finished there, he'd search every nook and cranny in the Collective until he found his daughter. God have mercy on anyone who got in his way.

CHAPTER 9

ATMO BURN

Devil Town, Spate
Throttle

THROTTLE WOKE with a jolt in the middle of the night. She could've sworn she heard the door open, but she could see nothing in the darkness.

When someone touched her hand, she nearly tumbled out of bed.

"Sh," a little girl whispered. "They're always listening."

"Lily?" Throttle asked softly. "Is that you?"

The girl didn't answer, though Throttle suspected she was nodding.

"My father said your father killed my grandmother. Is that true?"

Throttle frowned, not quite sure how best to respond. The wrong answer could send running the only hope Throttle had of escape. She decided to answer simply and honestly. "Yes."

"Did you know her?"

Throttle shook her head. "No. I only heard stories about her."

"Was she like my father?"

Again, Throttle struggled for the right answer. "Yes. I suppose she was."

A long silence followed. "Then, your father can't be that bad."

Throttle nearly smiled. "No, he's not bad at all. He's a pretty good guy."

"I saw what my father did to my mother."

"What did he do?"

Silence blanketed the room for several seconds before she answered softly, "I don't want him to do that to me."

Throttle heard the little girl pad across the floor, and the door opened to a dimly lit hallway. After the door closed, Throttle lay in bed reliving their short conversation over and over. She was never quite sure what to make of it until Lily snuck into Throttle's room the next night, and the five nights after that.

———

Throttle walked across the room with Qelle's help. It was the sixth day in a row Axos and Qelle had stopped by Throttle's room—the sixth day Axos had turned on, and then off, her spinal implant. Each day, she opened up a little more to him. The arrogant stationmaster was so sure of his superior intelligence that he fell for Throttle's change of heart hook, line, and sinker.

Though, she had to admit, giving someone the power to walk was pretty damn persuasive.

"Excellent work. Now, try it on your own," Axos said. "Qelle, release her."

Qelle let go of Throttle's arm and stepped back.

Throttle wobbled, and nearly fell on the first step. Each step after that was slow and tentative. It took her nearly five minutes to walk the room. Once she completed a full circle, she looked up and grinned.

"You did it," Axos said.

Throttle took another step, but tripped on the rug and fell to her hands and knees. "Damn it."

Qelle rushed over to help her.

"Get away from her!" Axos stormed, knocking his chair over.

Qelle cowered in the corner.

Throttle remained on her knees, keeping a wary eye on Axos in the tense silence that followed. Qelle made herself as small as possible.

Axos reset the chair and took a seat. "Give it time, Halit," Axos said, as though he hadn't just had an outburst. "You've made great progress this week. At this rate, you could walk the station on your own within a month or two. Imagine Reyne's face if you walked up to him."

Throttle gave him a thoughtful look. "I really appreciate what you've done for me, but I don't know where he is. He came to Spate with me, but I haven't heard from him since we split."

"I know," Axos said. "But I think that once your legs get stronger, you can reach out to him. Perhaps call him to come pick you up."

She stared at her legs, then back up at Axos, and gave a small nod. "Yeah, I could do that."

He smiled. "I think we've made good progress. How would you like to have full use of your legs tonight?"

She beamed. "I'd like that."

"Enjoy the evening." Axos stood to leave.

"Can I get my clothes back?" Throttle asked, then added, "If it's not too much to ask, I mean. I feel a bit naked in these hospital gowns."

"I had those rags burned." He looked her up and down. "I

imagine you're about Qelle's size. She'll bring you something to wear."

Qelle nodded from where she stood in the corner.

"Thank you," Throttle said, but Qelle made no comment.

Axos left with Qelle trailing behind him.

Throttle plopped down on the bed and ran her hands down her legs, savoring every sensation. Every few minutes, she'd stand, walk a few steps, and then rest again.

Some time later, Qelle arrived with dinner.

"Hello, Qelle," Throttle said with a welcoming tone. She'd learned to treat the mouse gently, and Qelle had let down her guard. Throttle, on the other hand, knew to never let her guard down around the other woman. Axos had picked a woman with a naturally subservient personality, and he terrified Qelle. Throttle had no doubt Qelle went to her master each night after visiting Throttle to tell him everything.

"You doing okay?" Throttle asked.

"I'm fine. And you?" came Qelle's auto-response.

Throttle didn't answer, and Qelle didn't seem to expect her to. The woman set the tray down at the foot of the bed, lifted the bag she'd carried over her shoulder, and pulled out a bunch of iridescent blue material. "You're a little smaller than me. I think this dress will fit you."

Throttle cringed inwardly as she reached out and took the dress. "Thanks, I love it."

"How about you try it on? If it doesn't fit, I can find something else."

Throttle turned her back to Qelle, slipped off the hospital gown she wore, and slipped the gown over her head. She tugged up the low neckline. She felt even barer in this than she had in the hospital gown. She remembered that her legs worked, and she stood to finish dressing. The slinky gown slid down to her ankles, and she took a moment to savor the sensation of delicate fabric brushing against her skin.

Qelle seemed disappointed. "It's a bit loose and a bit long, but it's the smallest I had."

"It's perfect," Throttle said, reaching out and clasping Qelle's hand. "Thank you."

Qelle beamed, and then she looked down. "I'm afraid I had no undergarments or shoes that would fit you."

"It's okay. This is better than before."

"You look nice. I could do your hair sometime if you'd like."

"I'll think about." Throttle tried not to roll her eyes. *What's next? Have pedicures together?*

"Oh, I have your dinner," Qelle said, turning her attention back to the tray.

"Is it okay if you leave it?" Throttle asked. "I'm hungry, but it's just that I'm so excited to have time with my legs, I don't know if I could keep food down right now."

Qelle looked at the food as though trying to figure out what to do.

Throttle chuckled. "It's not like I could kill myself with a spoon."

"Of course not. It's just that it's lights out in another hour. I don't know if I can make it back tonight. Your room will smell if I leave the tray here all night."

"I'll be fine," Throttle said.

"All right," Qelle said. "I'll leave you be. I'm sure you're anxious to walk around your room more."

"You've got that right," Throttle said.

As Throttle watched Qelle leave, she felt sorry for the woman. Qelle Delta must have a horrific life, but there was nothing Throttle could do for her; not without risking her own life.

For the next hour, Throttle took small steps. In between mild exercises, she nibbled at her food and sipped her drink. When the lights went out, Throttle found herself in total darkness. She sat on the bed and reached out until she found the bowl of black hash.

Axos Wintsel was a Myrad. He never ate hash, let alone would have any idea it had more uses than for food. It was also the hair color of choice across the fringe, used to cover the most resistant grays. Throttle grabbed a handful of the hash and ran it through her light blonde hair. Without a mirror, she moved slowly to make sure she covered everything without staining her face. Her palms would be stained, but nobody looked at those. By the time she was finishing, the door unlocked and opened.

A young girl's silhouette stood in the doorway.

Throttle pushed to her feet, unsteady in her first steps, and then moving more smoothly across the floor. She'd exaggerated her clumsiness and weakness earlier. While she was in no way ready to jog, she felt somewhat steady on her feet now.

When she reached Lily, the little girl took Throttle's hand while clutching a teddy bear in her other arm. They walked down the empty hallway. She'd never been outside her room, and was counting on Lily to know where she was going. After several turns, Throttle was exhausted. Her legs burned at the unfamiliar use, but she pushed through. If they failed, she'd be dead by morning. Walking required all of Throttle's concentration and strength, and kept them at a slow pace, giving Throttle far too much time to begin doubting the escape plan.

"Qelle? Lily? What are you doing out past curfew?" a male voice called out behind them.

Throttle froze.

Lily looked over her shoulder. "I'm hungry. Qelle's getting me a snack, Mugsy."

"All right, but be quick about it. You know your father doesn't want you out and about after curfew."

Throttle exhaled, and they continued down the hallway. In the dim light, she could vaguely resemble Qelle from behind, with the dark hair and Qelle's gown. But if anyone got close, it'd be obvious she was no Qelle.

They reached the kitchen without running into a guard. The light suddenly dimmed. A feminine figure rose from behind the counter. Throttle tensed.

"We need to hurry," the woman said. "It won't take them long to realize something is up."

"This is Bree," Lily said. "She's coming with us."

Throttle nodded at the other woman, who returned the motion. Bree was dressed in a skin-tight dress with a deep neckline and high slit. Wearing too much makeup, she looked like every other prostitute in Devil Town.

Bree pulled out three breather masks and handed them out. "I have a cab waiting."

They put on their masks and rushed forward. Throttle tripped when she tried to walk faster, and Lily tried to steady her. Bree grabbed Throttle's other arm, and they headed out the back door.

Sure enough, an auto-cab sat outside. The trio piled into it. Throttle let out a sigh as soon as her weight was off her legs. Bree used her wrist comm to pay, and the cab pulled away from the curb.

Throttle looked at Lily. "Did you get the device?"

Lily frowned. "No. He carries it on him. He never puts it down."

Throttle forced herself to not look disappointed. "It's okay. You did good. You did a very brave thing back there."

Lily hugged her bear. "I just want to feel safe."

Bree wrapped a protective arm around the girl. "You'll be safe from him soon."

Throttle didn't voice her thoughts. Axos was obsessed with

Qelle—at least the visage of Qelle—and Lily was the only true remaining piece of Qelle. Not to mention his only daughter. She doubted he would ever quit searching for Lily.

When the docks grew near, Throttle felt hopeful. The stationmaster had the authority to shut down all cabs within Devil Town. That Axos hadn't, meant he didn't yet know of their escape. She didn't relax until the cab stopped and they exited. They couldn't be locked inside.

The trio hustled onto the dock, with Bree assisting Throttle. Excitement built within Throttle as they entered dock Hilo, the same dock she'd landed on when she'd first arrived on Spate. Would the *Gryphon* still be there? She craved to be behind the pilot panel again.

"It's in bay Nine," Bree said through her breather mask.

Disappointment lurched. The *Gryphon* was in bay Two, but bay Two now sat empty. What had happened to it? Had Axos already turned it over to the CUF? The *Gryphon* had been her legs for nearly her entire life. Knowing she was well and truly separated from it felt akin to Axos turning off her implant.

Bree pointed. "There it is."

Throttle saw the small ship, and bit back her disappointment. It was a Chital model, too small to even have been christened with its own name. Chitals were small cruisers, one of the cheapest ships one could buy. Its small navigational engine would have to work hard just to break out of Spate's atmosphere. If the CUF chased them, they wouldn't stand a chance.

At this time of night, the dock stood nearly empty. They came across a couple of dock personnel who were busy working on a ship a few bays down.

When they reached the Chital's ramp, a guard from the bay next to theirs noticed them. "Bree? That you?"

As he headed toward them, Bree patted Lily's shoulder. "Hustle inside, sweetie."

Bree let go of Throttle and walked toward him.

"What are you doing on Shane's ship?" He wagged his eyebrows. Making a lascivious expression wearing a breather mask made him look foolish. "Having a little rendezvous, are you?"

She gave a sensual shrug. "You know how he likes to try new things. He asked me to meet him here, so here I am."

"You naughty girl," the man said. When he noticed the little girl running up the ramp, he stomped toward Bree and grabbed her by the neck. "What're you doing with Mr. Wintsel's daughter?"

Bree couldn't speak, since she was being choked. She kneed him in the groin and he dropped her. She lay coughing on the ground, trying to push herself up.

He stayed bent over for a second or so, giving Throttle time to close the distance. When he returned to full height, he glared at Bree. "I'm not done with you." He turned toward the ship. He was so focused on Lily that he ignored Throttle.

Big mistake.

She hit him square in the temple. The man dropped instantly, and she fell on top of him. Spending a lifetime in a wheelchair had given her upper body strength few women possessed, but using her legs would take some practice.

Bree picked herself up and pulled a photon gun from his holster. She took a step back, pointed the gun at him, and fired.

At such close range, his chest cavity became a burned black hole. Death was instantaneous.

Bree glanced at Throttle. "Trust me, he deserves worse." Then Bree assisted Throttle up the ramp and into the ship. As Bree helped Throttle into the pilot's seat, she held out the ship's keycard. "I hope you're as good as your reputation."

Throttle took the card and slid it into the panel. "Don't worry. I could fly this piece of crap with my eyes closed." The systems came to life. She threw Bree a quick glance. "I'm guessing I shouldn't ask how you got the keycard?"

Bree jut out her chin. "Shane sleeps like a rock after he finishes."

"Oh." Throttle turned her focus back to the ship. "Make sure you're both buckled in tight. This model isn't exactly known for comfort."

She opened the comm channel.

"Dock control, this is Chital..." She had to look down at the panel to read its N-number. "...Myr-Five-Five-Bravo-Five-Four. Ready for departure."

"Chital Bravo-Five-Four, launch approved. Launch commences in sixty."

As the countdown numbers flashed in the upper right corner of her panel, Throttle ran full system checks. Several indicators flashed yellow. Throttle pursed her lips. Shane had been neglecting maintenance on his ship for way too long.

At ten seconds to go, she fired up the engine.

When the countdown hit zero, dock control reported, *"Chital Bravo-Five-Four, launch upon your command."*

"Dock control, launch Chital Bravo-Five-Four. Have a great day."

The dock's launch system shot the Chital upward at seven Gs, and the trio was thrown back in their seats. Throttle could handle thirteen Gs, so she had no problem maintaining manual control of the nav engine.

The ship vibrated and sounded like it was going to fall apart as it flew upward through the Spaten atmosphere. *Hold together, hold together, hold together,* Throttle thought to herself as she looked at the space above them for any signs of CUF ships.

When the Chital broke through the atmosphere and entered the calm blackness of space, the ship's vibrations smoothed out, and Throttle exhaled and patted the panel. "Good job."

She pulled up the cosmic charts and scanned for CUF patrols, finding one four thousand clicks off her stern. Far enough away it couldn't have a visual, but close enough it could run them down if needed. She would've preferred it to be twice that distance out.

She turned to her two passengers. Bree had her eyes closed and still clenched her armrests. Lily had her eyes wide open as she stared open-mouthed out into space. She still clutched her teddy bear.

"How're you holding up, Lily?" Throttle asked.

The girl turned to her, and for the first time since Throttle had met her, she smiled. "I'm safe now."

Throttle returned the smile. She flew the ship at max speed, burning its juice, in order to put more distance between them and the patrol ship. They'd just passed between Spate's two moons when Bree asked, "Where are we going?"

Throttle thought long and hard. Playa was her first choice. It was the emergency rendezvous point and where Reyne would go. She glanced at Lily. Many of those refugees at Tulan Base had been abused by the CUF, and Myrads in particular. Lily's bluish skin was a bulls-eye for anyone with a vendetta, though she knew Reyne would protect the girl. On the other hand, Sixx was on Myr right now. He'd return to Terra, and who knew how long he'd be there. He'd been searching for Qelle, and needed to see Lily. Throttle didn't like heading in that direction, but it was their best option.

"We're going to Terra," she announced finally.

Bree sat upright. "Terra? But that's where the war is!"

"It is. But it's also the one place where we can protect Lily from Axos." She was about to elaborate, when a terrible burn spread down her spine and into her legs, followed by familiar coldness.

"What's wrong?" Lily asked.

Throttle exhaled. "He knows."

Bree and Lily both bore the same expression of wide-eyed terror.

Throttle eyed the smaller moon and cranked the ship into its orbit. "Don't worry. I have a few tricks up my sleeve."

Once the moon's dark side enveloped the small ship, she cut the engine, turned off the comms, and lowered the life support system to minimum. "Bree, find us some blankets. It's going to get chilly in here."

When Bree looked at her, confused, Throttle elaborated. "Patrol ships scan for energy signatures. We're not broadcasting enough of a signature for their systems to pick us up."

"But what if they see us?" Bree countered.

"They'd have to get within a couple hundred clicks to get a visual on us. And as long as we stay on the dark side, nothing will reflect off the ship. They'd have an easier time finding a needle in a haystack."

Bree thought for a moment, and then seemed to snap back to attention. She unbuckled and moved around the small cabin. The only blankets were on the ship's two fold-out bunks. The trio huddled together as the temperatures quickly dropped.

"How long do we have to wait?" Lily asked in a soft voice.

Throttle shivered. "As long as we have to."

Her implant went on again, only to be shut off a few seconds later. Each time, she bit through the pain. She knew Axos was torturing her on purpose, taking out his anger on her from a distance. That temper of his had killed Sixx's wife, along with how many other innocents. Throttle clenched her teeth. He could torture her all he wanted. He wasn't going to kill her. But she sure as hell was going to kill him.

CHAPTER 10

OLD FRIENDS

Space, on the way to Terra
Heid

HEID SAT in her quarters on board the *Arcadia*, staring at the blank comm screen. She'd been staring for a good ten minutes, trying to build her confidence. This wasn't the first time she'd called Barrett since she'd broken ties with the Forces, but this was the first time she'd be testing their friendship.

She took a deep breath. Then she dialed the number, using an encrypted scrambler.

He answered within a few seconds. "Hello, Gabi."

She smiled. "Hello, Barrett. You look good." He did. The blue commandant's uniform looked right on him, and he'd always had a natural poise and confidence that seemed to exude from him in every interaction.

"And you look stunning as always." He cocked his head. "I believe this is the first time I've seen you out of uniform. Even back at the Academy, I don't remember ever seeing you out of an approved uniform."

She glanced down at the simple clothes she now wore. Her shirt had been hand-sewn by a Nova colonist as a gift for her coming to Nova Colony's aid. She wore it as a reminder of whom she was fighting for. She turned her attention back to Barrett. "I won't take much of your time. I know the longer we talk, the greater the risk of having our comms intercepted. Do you remember the conversation we had the last time we spoke?"

He nodded. "I do, and I still stand by my belief in equality for all. As do the other two. We all believe what you did was courageous, but you'll always be on the run as long as you're alive and the *Arcadia* flies."

"Don't worry about me," she said. "I can take care of myself."

"I have no doubt," he said.

She inhaled. "I'm sure you saw Stationmaster Faulk's broadcast."

"*Everyone* has seen the broadcast. Ausyar has ordered the entire Armada to be sent to the fringe, though we're still awaiting direction on how the Forces will respond."

"And where are you to take the *Littorio*?" Heid asked.

"I'm off to Terra, leading a complement of two frigates and six destroyers," he said.

She lifted her chin. "Good. I need support at Terra."

"I see." His lips thinned. "Exactly what kind of support do you have in mind?"

She swallowed. "Whatever support it takes to ensure Rebus Station remains in the hands of Terrans and not Ausyar."

He took a deep breath. "You were able to take the *Arcadia* because you'd spent years hand-picking your crew for that precise reason. Nearly all my crew are citizens, many of them Myrad. The Forces have changed since you left, Gabriela. Dromadiers will turn in their bunkmates at the slightest whisper of rebellion."

She swallowed. "I suspected as much."

He held up a hand. "However, if Ausyar were no longer corps general, I could be of great support to the colonies' quest for independence."

Chills flitted across her skin at the sudden hope sprouting inside her. "I believe my friends and I may be of assistance in making that happen. Your support means more than you'll ever know, Barrett."

He shrugged. "We go back a long way. You know you can count on me when it matters."

She smiled. "I know. And the others?"

"There's not a single warship commandant who wants to fire upon colonists. Smith and Lyness are both off to Darios, along with much of the remainder of the Armada. They, too, look for opportunities to bring peace to the Collective."

She frowned. "Why Darios? I thought Sol Base was firmly under CUF control, since the blight was destroyed."

"It is. But many other Darion colonies have banded together and have surrounded Sol Base. They keep picking off ground forces. They seem hell-bent on taking Sol Base, even if they have to blow the docks to take it."

Pride stirred. "Good for them. That blight wiped out their largest city, and they know the Myrads were behind it. Who can blame them for wanting anyone associated with Myr off their planet?"

He gave her a knowing look. "We both know the Collective will never willingly give up Darios. The planet's food feeds seventy percent of the Collective."

"The Collective should've considered that before they started treating colonists like second-class citizens," she retorted.

He held up his hands. "I agree, but I'm saying that out of all the colonies, the Collective depends on Darios."

"Then, we'll pry Darios out of the Collective's cold, dead hands if we have to," she said.

He frowned. "Let's hope things don't come to that." She heard a chime on his end, and he glanced away. "I'll talk to you soon." The screen went blank.

She gripped the table to hold her anxiety in check. She'd taken a great risk in calling Barrett, but the Campaign needed more support if it were to succeed.

Commandant Barrett Anders had been her study partner at the CUF military academy, and they'd remained close friends throughout their careers. He'd even dated her roommate, Lina, for a couple months. She realized that she should've told him Lina was currently sitting in prison, courtesy of Ausyar. News like that would've likely erased any doubts he might still be having about helping the Campaign.

She pushed off from her desk. They'd be reaching their destination within four hours. It was time she met with her crew. They needed to understand what they were about to face at Terra.

Torrent Headquarters, Terra
Critch

"REBUS DOCK CONTROL informed me the *Scorpia* has been captured and is sitting in their docks," Hari announced as she walked into the lounge where Seda and Critch sat drinking whiskey.

Critch's eye twitched. "And her crew?"

She lowered her face. "Executed. Rumor is they were drifted from a frigate."

"That's a loss to the Campaign," Seda said. "The *Scorpia* was a good ship and crew."

"The best." Critch took a long drink. The *Scorpia* was the newest ship in the feared specter fleet—the fleet of pirates turned torrents. He'd overseen the ship's design, and had hired every crewmember back when he was a pirate. He set down his empty glass. "How about we take it back?"

Seda thought for a moment, rubbing his right shoulder where

his prosthetic arm connected to his skin. "It feels too soon to make a move for the docks."

"We take the docks, we take Rebus Station. Ausyar will be forced to launch a new offensive or negotiate."

Seda cocked his head. "Corps General Ausyar is not the type to negotiate, and I'm not comfortable forcing him into a corner."

Critch rapped his fingers on the chair's armrest. "We also can't maintain guerrilla tactics. We'll run out of resources and soldiers long before the CUF does."

"I agree with Critch," Hari said. "The only reason we took the warehouse district is because the CUF is under public scrutiny. Citizen support is currently in our favor, but who knows how long that will last, with the Collective propaganda machine skewing all the news. If we can take Rebus Station with minimal loss of innocent lives, then we have a chance at having an honest negotiation with Ausyar or Parliament."

Seda refilled his and Critch's empty glasses, and poured a glass for Hari. "There's a way I can do that, but—" He cursed. "This is going to slash my revenue streams." He looked up at the pair watching him. "There are only two reasons the Collective cares about Terra."

"Your plants provide over ninety percent of the fuel used for interplanetary travel," Hari said.

Critch added, "And we're sitting right smack in between the citizen worlds and their darling garden colony, Darios."

Seda nodded. "I have direct control over one of those things."

Hari's eyes widened. "You're not going to turn the juice plants over to the Collective, are you?"

Seda belted out a laugh. "No. I'm going to blow them all." He then scowled, as if the words had a bad taste in his mouth, and he downed his drink and threw the glass across the room. It hit the wall and shattered into hundreds of tiny shards.

Critch's gaze narrowed. "That'll hurt our fleet as much as it'll hurt the CUF's. Everyone will be running off solar power only within months, if not weeks. That means no more jump capabilities."

Seda shook his head. "The CUF burns through exponentially more juice than all general aviation combined. It'll cripple them before it cripples us—both by losing jump capabilities as well as serving a blow to the economy. I have new plant locations mapped that haven't yet been reviewed by Parliament. I also have the expertise on hand to rebuild a plant. We can have new juice flowing for colonists within two years. The CUF has no such resources, and after the stranglehold the CUF has had on Rebus Station, no Terran would work for the Collective, no matter how well they paid."

"They can force them to work," Hari said. "The Collective has supported indentured servitude for decades. If you take away one of their most precious resources, you may push them over the ledge into legalizing slavery."

"The declaration of independence has been made," Seda said. "If the Collective moves into slavery, the remaining colonies will join a single cause rather than all fight for themselves. It would only strengthen the Fringe Liberation Campaign. The CUF cannot sustain a war spread out over four planets and an asteroid belt, especially without jump speed. It would take them months to move ships among planets, and years to move from one end of the fringe to the other. Entire wars could be fought and won during such time."

"Do it," Critch said. "It levels the battlefield, and the colonists have the upper hand planetside. I don't like the idea of having the *Honorless*'s wings clipped, but we've been at a stalemate, more or less, for the past year. We take a block here and lose a block there. This way, we can push the war to the next front, whatever that becomes."

Seda turned to Hari. "You know I've always depended on your counsel. I want to know you're with me on this."

Her features were tight and her lips thin, but she gave a small nod. "I'm with you. Always."

Seda opened the computer panel on his desk. He looked nauseous as he entered codes into the system. "I knew the plants were always at risk to be taken by the CUF," he said as he continued typing. "Which is why I established safeguards and prepared procedures for all staff."

He breathed deeply, tapped a final button, and then leaned back. "Every active plant listed on Parliament's register of fuel operations will self-destruct in ninety minutes. All staff employed as of today will be credited five years' salary in their bank accounts. That will hopefully be enough to encourage them to work for me again after we're free from the Collective."

Critch walked over to the bar and grabbed a new glass and filled it. He handed it to Seda. "Now, we wait."

Two hours later, every juice plant on Terra melted. Critch had expected massive explosions, but evidently Seda had taken more environmentally-friendly measures to disable the plants without firework shows.

Seda made no news announcement, instead waiting to see how Ausyar and Parliament responded. He had sent out a company-wide communication, which stated the plants were being demolished to prevent hostile takeover. Critch liked to think Seda's employees would've done the same thing had they been in his shoes.

The trio waited another two hours before anything happened.

Seda's comm channel lit up. "Corbin, what do you have?"

"There's been no change to the CUF formation. There are two warships, four frigates, and twelve destroyers, all in standard orbital formation. But it looks like every gunship and transport that was on Terra's surface is launching, and they're not wasting their time returning to the fleet."

"Expand your scans to include two quadrants out from Terra's orbit. Keep a close eye on every CUF ship out there, and let me know the moment you see one change course even a tenth of a degree," Seda said and disconnected the comm.

Hari's wrist comm chimed, and she read a message. She looked up, startled. "The CUF is evacuating Rebus Station. They've relinquished control of the docks and are in the process of departing. My contact says colonists are cheering in the streets, and Dock Control is launching CUF ships as soon as they are boarded. They expect to have the docks cleared within an hour." She grabbed her chest. "Seda, you did it. We've reclaimed Rebus Station!"

Critch grumbled. "Damn. I was itching for a fight."

"You may get one yet." Seda steepled his fingers as he eyed Critch and Hari, the high-tech artificial limb nearly identical to his left hand. "I won't be comfortable until Ausyar and his fleet are at least a million clicks from Terra's orbit."

Critch pushed to his feet.

"Where are you headed?" Seda asked.

"There'll be chaos on the streets, now the CUF is gone. I'm going to lead a team in to help secure the docks. We'll move in the morning. If Ausyar hasn't blown Rebus Station to bits by then, we should be in the clear."

"Maybe, if you're lucky, you'll find a couple of droms who didn't make it off-world," Seda said with sarcasm.

"Maybe," Critch replied without a hint of sarcasm.

▭

It was in the early morning, an hour before the sun came up, when Critch took four teams with him to secure the docks. They drove through town in four gray trucks, where colonists still partied in the streets. They had to weave through the crowds and passed-out drunks. Bottles crunched under the tires. Partyers held up drinks and cheered at the vehicles when they saw who was inside. The crowd began to chant, "Fender, Fender!" over and over again, as if Critch were some kind of legend. One woman bared her chest, which brought on more cheers.

"Do we have to stop for the infamous Drake Fender to sign autographs?" Birk asked with a sly grin.

"Keep driving," Critch growled. He gave a lazy wave in acknowledgement of the cheers.

He was surprised to see there'd been no riots, though he knew they would come. Rebus Station was currently in a state of anarchy, which meant lawlessness, which meant there would be those who'd have no qualms about taking advantage of their neighbors if it served their selfish needs.

He suspected Seda and he would have to expend torrent resources keeping the colony safe until Rebus Station could reorganize its own police force. All that assumed the Collective was truly turning control of the colony back to the colonists. Critch had his doubts.

By the time they reached the docks, night gave way to morning dawn. It'd taken them longer to arrive than Critch had planned, though he supposed they weren't on a schedule for this mission. Critch keyed his team on his wrist comm. "This goes down how we planned. Maddox, your team has the commercial docks. Nat, your team's on the cargo docks. Alex, your team's on the general aviation docks. My team's taking the Collective docks. Report back in one hour. Time check is 0547."

Double-clicks came back from each team lead in acknowledgement of the plan, and the trucks pulled away in a starburst pattern as each team headed to its docks.

Critch had chosen the Collective docks since they posed the most risk. If Ausyar had left squads, they would most likely be found here. Dock Control had reported an all-clear, but Critch had to see for himself that the CUF had cleared out.

The Collective docks were three rows of parallel docks. Birk drove them slowly down the first row. It was entirely empty. Not a single ship remained. "So far, so good," Birk said, and he picked up speed.

"Sure you don't want us to walk the docks?" James asked from the back seat.

Critch turned around. "Not this time. Today's just a quick pass through to make sure they didn't leave any nasty surprises behind. We'll be back after the fleet leaves orbit."

The second row was empty except for two small cargo haulers. When he saw the *Faulk Industries* logo on the hulls, he suspected they'd been seized by the CUF and abandoned when the Ausyar cleared out his ground forces. The CUF had no need for civilian ships in their armada, but they often seized colonist ships and sold them on auction to citizens. Critch had lost two pirate ships to the CUF in his earlier days before he'd learned how to better avoid detection.

"Seda will like having those back," Critch said, and Birk continued on.

When they drove down the third row of docks, Critch felt a weight lift off his chest. In one of the last docking bays stood his missing specter.

Birk pointed. "Hey, that's the *Scorpia*."

Critch nodded. It was good to see her, though he preferred to see her crew with her. He turned to Birk. "She's yours if you want her."

Birk's jaw dropped. "Mine? But—"

"But nothing. You've been on my team for ten years now. It's time you had your own ship. Then you don't have to sneak your girlfriend onto my ship anymore."

Birk stuttered for a couple of seconds before he gulped and said, "Thanks. This is the first time anyone's ever given me something."

Critch scowled. "Aw, damn it. You're not going to cry on me now, are you?"

"No," he replied quickly, but his voice was shaky.

The six other team members started cracking jokes from the back seat.

"Quit messing with me guys," Birk said, "or else I won't ask any of you losers to be on the *Scorpia*'s crew."

"Are you going to rename it *Pinky*?" Laughs erupted.

Birk held up his pinky finger, which was missing the top inch. "Hey, it was a serious injury."

That really got them going.

Critch enjoyed the camaraderie. These people were his family, and he looked forward to the day the CUF stopped trying to kill them. Not like he expected that to ever happen.

He motioned to the tower that stood in the center of all the docks. "Let's head to the Rebus Station Dock Control tower and check in with them."

The jokes continued as Birk approached the front of the tower without slowing down. Critch braced himself against the dash. He'd worked alongside Birk for enough years that he could practically read the younger man's mind. Birk applied the brakes hard, and all six men in the back seats rammed into the ones in front of them. Jokes turned into groans and curses.

Critch shook his head, though humor tugged at his lips. He stepped out of the truck and headed for the tower. His wrist comm chimed, and he saw a message from Seda. *"Orbital forma-*

tion is reconfiguring. The Unity *is powering up. Get out of Rebus Station now!"*

He looked up to see massive phase cannon blasts raining fire down from the sky. Critch's eyes grew wide as he stared at the sky, expecting to be disintegrated in the next instant. But the blasts didn't hit near the docks. Instead, they hit many miles away, far from Rebus Station. Critch's blood ran cold. He ran around the truck to see for himself.

Where a mountain had once stood proudly on the horizon, there was nothing but flat land.

Broken Mountain was gone.

Critch fell to his knees.

Hundreds of innocent refugees would've been eating breakfast in the mountain's caves. Fires hotter than the circles of hell would've poured through the tunnels like an insatiable dragon. Most would've died instantly. *Most.*

The men, women, and children inside never stood a chance.

There was no strategic advantage gained by Ausyar bombing a refugee camp. If anything, Ausyar would lose citizen support for the action. The corps general had bombed Broken Mountain purely out of an emotional need for retaliation.

The cold chills coursing through Critch's body enveloped his heart in hard ice. He pressed a hand on the ground to push himself to his feet. He remembered the threat he'd made to the drom when they'd reclaimed the warehouse district. Ausyar fought without honor. Critch had no problem doing the same.

CHAPTER 12

REPERCUSSIONS

Space, three quadrants out from Terra
Heid

"WILL, initiate reverse engines. Cut forward movement. Let's not step on the welcome mat quite yet," Heid ordered from her chair on the bridge.

"Aye, aye, Captain," Will responded.

The slightest change in the constant hum of the *Arcadia's* engines was all that could be noticed when the ship was brought to a standstill.

"What do we do now?" Sylvian asked.

"We wait," Heid said. "Nolin, run scans on the ships in Terran orbit. Mark the *Unity* and her complement. I want to know the exact location of every CUF ship near Terra."

"Aye, aye, Captain," Nolin said.

The CUF had never had to fight any significant space marine fleet before, and because of that, the armada had been kept small, with military budgets supporting ground forces, gunships, and patrol ships far more than warships.

While the CUF armada still dwarfed the specter fleet, the *Arcadia* changed the game. A Titan-class warship, the *Arcadia* dwarfed every other CUF ship except for its equals—the *Unity* and the *Littorio.*

At the academy, she'd devoured books covering the Jovian War. In its epic space battles, the lunar, Mars, and Europa colonies had fought Earth's massive space marine force for independence.

Earth had treated its colonies much like Alluvia and Myr did now. The difference now was, the Collective didn't have an enormous force like Earth had had. Too far from the Jovian system to worry about massive cosmic battles, the CUF designed its military strategy around two roles—a traffic cop to police fringe ships, and a guard dog over the colonies. The armada contained many gunships and patrol ships, but few warships, frigates, and destroyers. Its energy-based weapons, such as phase cannons and photon guns, could rain down terrifying damage on land-based targets. The same weapons posed far less danger in the vacuum of space, where a shot fired could be tracked from thousands of clicks away, giving its opponents hours to change course to avoid hitting a blast that could only travel in a straight line.

The *Arcadia* had been a typical CUF warship, armed only with energy weapons. But Heid had added armaments that could wreak havoc on a warship and break apart anything smaller, like a frigate or a destroyer. She both dreaded and looked forward to using them. She mused the *Arcadia* looked more like a pirate ship now than a military ship, and she felt pride in its new look. She wondered what that thought said about her.

"Captain," Nolin said, "the *Unity* just fired its phase cannons at the planet."

Heid clenched her armrests. "What was the target?"

He answered several seconds later. "I have the coordinates." He turned around. "It was Broken Mountain."

She collapsed back in her chair. Broken Mountain, first a temporary home for those freed from the Citadel, had become the sanctuary of any refugee found homeless or whose life was in peril.

"Sylvian, connect me to Terran headquarters."

A moment later, Hari's distraught image appeared on Heid's screen.

"What's going on down there, Hari?" Heid demanded.

Hari yelled a command to someone offscreen, and then turned back to Heid. "The CUF evacuated Rebus Station last night. And they've just bombed Broken Mountain. We have no details on the severity, but from visuals, it looks like a total loss."

"Put me through to Seda and Critch."

"Hold on. Seda's en route to Broken Mountain, and Critch is still at the docks."

Heid's screen split into three visuals. One showed Hari looking away. Critch joined next. His image background was shaky, like he was walking. Seda joined a second later.

Heid spoke first. "What do you know so far about the attack?"

Seda answered. "It came from the *Unity*, likely in retaliation for me blowing all my juice plants."

Heid's lips parted in shock at the news, but she quickly regained her composure. "Do you anticipate more attacks?"

Critch spoke first. "If the fleet departs orbit, then it was a parting shot. If they stay in orbit, I'd lay bets they'll hit more targets."

Her jaw tightened. "I can be within firing range of the *Unity* in under thirty minutes." She took a quick breath. "Do you want me to attack the *Unity*?"

"Yes," Critch said as a matter of fact.

"Belay that," Seda said quickly and loudly. "The situation's far too tenuous. Bringing the *Arcadia* into orbit will add gas to the fire. That will guarantee another attack. We need to see what Ausyar will do next."

"Hari," Critch said. "Has the fleet shown any indication of breaking orbit yet?"

Hari looked off screen again. "No. They are still holding in the same orbital configuration. Wait. I take it back. It looks like the two frigates have broken off."

"Captain," Nolin yelled, "we have two frigates on an intercept course."

"Shields up," Heid commanded with frustration. The *Arcadia* must've been caught on a scan, something she hadn't expected. She turned back to her comm panel. "They're on their way to me. I'll report in after we deal with them." With that, she hung up the comm and turned her attention back to the bridge.

"How far out?" she asked.

"Fifteen thousand clicks," Nolin said. "They're increasing speed, and have raised their shields."

Heid hit her internal comm. "Jovo, activate missiles one and two."

"Activating missiles one and two, Captain," came Jovovich's reply.

She turned to Luther. "You have two missiles, Luther. Make each one count."

"I will." His hard gaze relayed how serious he was. Heid, like the rest of her crew who'd served in the CUF, had no experience with projectiles. They'd only been trained on energy weapons. Luther, a torrent from the Uprising, had extensive experience with every type of projectile weapon from machine guns to guided missile systems. She prayed his skills hadn't rusted too much in twenty years.

"Ten thousand clicks," Nolin said. "We're in photon range."

"Prepare for evasive maneuvers," Heid ordered. "Sylvian, ping them. Warn them that if they fire upon us, we will attack."

A second later. "Ping sent."

"Five thousand clicks. They've fired phase cannons!" Nolin announced. "I'm feeding trajectories now."

As soon as the trajectories were entered into the system, Will banked the ship to avoid the blasts with plenty of distance between them.

The frigates fired again, and the process repeated. This time, the distance between the ship and blasts was smaller.

"Three thousand clicks," Nolin said.

"Will, I need you to line up nose to nose with those frigates," Luther said.

"Hold on," Will said as his hands flew over the controls. "Okay. How's that?"

"Almost...yes, right there." Luther fired both guided missiles, one right after the other.

Each frigate quit firing as it maneuvered to avoid the new threat. They reacted to the missiles like they would photon blasts, which cost them. They banked to evade the missiles. As the missiles passed in between the two frigates, Luther exploded them, and shrapnel flew out from each missile in a 180-degree arc. Shrapnel cut through energy shields like butter, and pierced the hulls.

Projectiles weren't showy like phase cannons, but they got the job done more easily. With their hulls compromised in hundreds of small places, each frigate was losing crucial oxygen and heat too fast to replenish. Both ships turned and blasted back toward the fleet. Heid wondered if they'd make it back before their crews perished. She never enjoyed seeing lives lost, but she had no problem in seeing it done if it meant protecting her people.

Let them come.

CHAPTER 13

COMPLICATIONS

REYNE ENTERED orbit on the opposite side of Terra from where the CUF fleet sat above Rebus Station. He was surprised to find no drones or ships preventing him from landing. Of course, to leave, he needed the space docks, and the CUF sat in position to make a shooting gallery of anything that launched from the docks.

Fortunately, the CUF didn't know about Seda Faulk's secret spaceport, which had become the torrent headquarters on Terra. Once the *Gryphon* broke the atmosphere, Reyne kept the ship at an altitude of twenty thousand meters so he could maintain a decent speed and not fight turbulence on his trip halfway around the world.

Even pushing the engines, it took another four hours for the *Gryphon* to reach Seda's runway. He tapped the comm and announced across the ship, "Prepare for landing."

"I don't see it yet," Wen, a new torrent from Nova Colony, said from the seat Sixx usually sat in.

"Trust me, it's there," Reyne said. With a holographic canopy above the property, the spaceport looked like a rocky pasture. Reyne had been in and out of there before, though each time he brought the ship through the holographic ground was an unpleasant adrenaline rush.

As the ship sped toward what looked like rocky ground, Wen sucked in a breath.

Reyne held his breath too, until the ship passed through the camouflage and the spaceport came into full view. "It's there," he said on an exhale.

He'd sent an encrypted ping as soon as he'd entered orbit, to announce his arrival. When he saw a docking bay with a green light, he maneuvered the *Gryphon* into position and initiated the docking sequence. The ship lowered into the bay with a screeching thud, and Reyne winced. He glanced back at Wen. "I'm a bit rusty."

"I'm not complaining," Wen replied. "We're still alive, aren't we?"

"*I'm shutting down engines,*" Boden's voice came through the comms.

Reyne tapped his comm. "We're here. Welcome to Terra. Grab your bags and prepare to exit."

Wen stood. "I guess I'd better go clear out my bunk then."

"See you outside," Reyne said without looking back. He initiated the shutdown sequence, and the panel displayed the status of each system as it shut down in order. When the panel went blank, he unbuckled his seatbelt and stood.

He rubbed his stiff fingers and stretched his back. Every joint complained at lack of movement for so many hours. In his younger days, he could sit for an entire day without any problems. But he was sixty-seven now. If he were a citizen, he'd be in the prime of his life, but in the fringe, sixty-seven made him downright *old*.

He entered a code to lock down the *Gryphon*'s systems, and headed off the bridge. In the hallway, the dozen fresh-faced torrents stood at the door, ready to exit. Though, calling them "fresh-faced" was a stretch. Most were still skin-and-bones, and a few were up there in age with Reyne.

"Coming through," Reyne said as he weaved through the ragtag group. He opened the door and exited first. He stood off to the side as the rest walked down the ramp. A few were a bit wobbly as their bodies adjusted to the shift from the reduced gravity Reyne kept the *Gryphon* at to Terra's 1.2g.

"New arrivals, over here." A man waved at the crowd, and the passengers migrated in that direction.

Reyne noticed Sixx standing at the end of the dock, his arms crossed over his chest and a smile on his face. Reyne smiled back, and strode toward his second-in-command.

"Took you long enough to make it back here," Sixx said as Reyne approached.

They embraced in a bear hug.

Reyne stepped back. "It's good to see you."

Reyne could see the stress and fatigue behind his friend's features. "I heard about the Myr trip. I'm sorry that you didn't find what you were looking for."

Sixx waved him off. "It's been eleven years. What should I expect?"

"You should expect answers," Reyne said. "Any husband deserves that."

He blew out a breath. "The deeper I go, the more of a mess it becomes. I finally found a servant who recognized Qelle's picture. She said she'd seen her a few months back at the Smithton flower market." He held out a hand as though he wanted to make a fist. "Then later that same day, I came across another servant who not only recognized Qelle's picture but also said she knew her, and that Qelle had been dead for six years." He shook his head. "I don't know what to do. All I know is that until I'm positive Qelle is gone, I can't quit looking for her."

"We," Reyne said. "*We* won't quit looking for her."

Boden came up. "Ah, look what the cat dragged in."

Reyne couldn't tell which man looked more tired: the thief who'd had his wife stolen from him, or the recovering drug addict who'd spent time in a sweet soy den.

Sixx didn't make a witty comeback. Instead, he looked over Boden's shoulder. "Where's Throttle?"

No answer came.

Sixx's eyes narrowed as he looked from Reyne to Boden. Boden lowered his head and walked off without a word. Sixx turned back to Reyne. "What happened?"

"We believe droms picked her up at the docks in Devil Town."

Sixx took a step back like he'd been shot, and then paced in a small circle. Reyne knew exactly how his friend felt. Sixx had been a part of the crew since Throttle had been a child. He'd been a big brother to her, and would take her loss as hard, if not harder, than Reyne was taking it.

Sixx stopped. "Is she still alive?" His voice cracked.

"I think so," Reyne said, and then added a hard, "Yes. Nothing's been on the news." They both knew what Reyne had meant by that statement. Throttle was part of an infamous crew. If the CUF had her, she'd be publicly executed. That they had seen no news of an execution gave Reyne hope. "Vym's sent out for word on her whereabouts. We'll find her."

Sixx furled his brow, unconvinced.

"We'll find her," Reyne repeated, harder.

"We'll find her. We'll find both of them." Sixx clapped Reyne on the shoulder, and the pair began to walk slowly to the hangar Boden was entering.

When they reached the hangar door, Reyne inhaled deeply, for the first time noticing the fresh Terran air. "When this is all said and done, we're going to take a very long vacation somewhere very far from any sort of trouble."

Sixx grunted. "Don't forget, I still have that biome kit. I plan to find myself a nice little moon somewhere and set up a nice little terraformed ranch for myself when this is all done."

Reyne smirked. "You'd go crazy on a moon by yourself with nothing to steal."

He shrugged. "Maybe I'm ready to try something else."

With that, he held the door open for Reyne and then followed the captain inside.

It'd been a year since Reyne had been at Seda Faulk's personal retreat. That a single person could own something most colonies couldn't afford hinted at the massive fortune the man had attained from his business enterprises. Easily the richest of all colonists, Seda's wealth surpassed that of many citizens. Without Seda's support for the Fringe Liberation Campaign, the CUF would've quashed the rebellion within the first weeks. As it stood, Seda had given the fringe a fighting chance.

Knowing that both the CUF and the Founders would try multiple assassination attempts, they'd tried to keep Seda hidden from the public eye. That was a task proving to be impossible.

Sixx and Reyne walked through the massive hangar to the rooms at the other end. When they walked into the lounge, Seda and Critch—who'd been talking with Heid via a wall screen—both stopped and turned. They stood and approached Reyne.

Seda reached Reyne first, and they clasped forearms. "I'm glad you could make it. Did the fleet in orbit cause any trouble for you?"

"Strangely, not a peep," Reyne answered.

"That's what I was expecting." Seda stepped back. "There's a lot we need to catch you up on."

Critch clasped Reyne's forearm. "I won't kid you. Things are a mess."

"What else is new?" Reyne replied drily, and he took a seat.

Heid waved through the comm. "It's good to see you, Reyne."

He gave her a small nod. "Good to see you, too, Gabriela. I hear you've been keeping Vym busy."

"Yes, a third of production has been switched to preparing the colony ship."

"What?" Seda and Critch asked at the same time.

She glanced at the other men in the room. "I'm working with Vym to rebuild and stock the *Matador* for a colonization mission. I'll send you the plans, but I know we have more pressing matters today."

"You've repurposed the *Matador*?" Critch asked through narrowed eyes. "We're going to need that ship to transport supplies to the colonies. This is no time to talk about colonizing more worlds. You know the amount of resources that takes away from the Campaign?"

"The Campaign is why we need to talk about colonizing new worlds *now* rather than later," she said.

"We shouldn't even be thinking about colonization," Critch countered.

Heid glared. "Have you always been this hardheaded?"

"No," Critch replied. "I've become more laid back."

She blew out a breath. "We have so many refugees to resettle, and many of these refugees want a fresh start—not on an established colony, but somewhere new. This is a chance for the fringe to start fresh, without the Collective's shadow."

"Without juice, the *Matador* will take decades to reach new solar systems with habitable worlds. That means it'll need to be a generation ship, not just a transport ship," Seda said.

Heid frowned. "I heard about the plants. That puts a crimp on the plans, but we can work around it."

"How will you find a crew?" Critch asked. "No one's going to want to be a bus driver for the rest of their life."

Heid lifted her chin. "I'm going to captain the ship. And I've already received the names of several volunteers who want to join my crew."

"You?" Critch asked, incredulous. "We need you here, for the Campaign. You can't—"

"Yes, I *can*," she interrupted. "My mind is already made up. As soon as we have a peace treaty, I'll captain the *Matador*. I see it as the most important command I'll ever take. Don't you see? I'll be shepherding humankind to a new solar system. We messed things up in the Jovian and Centauri systems. Maybe I can help get things right in the third system."

Critch waved her off. "We'll talk about this later. You were right before. We have bigger things to cover, starting with what the hell is the *Arcadia* doing in a face-off against the fleet about Rebus Station?"

"I didn't anticipate their scans picking us up," she said.

"You shouldn't even be here," Critch said. "We can't risk losing our only warship."

"What good is a warship if it's not used?" she answered, sounding exasperated.

"One warship facing off against two warships, each with their own complement? Exactly how is *that* level?" Critch demanded.

"The *Arcadia* can hold her own," Heid replied with confidence. "Two frigates are out of commission."

Critch waved a hand. "Oh, great. That only leaves two warships, two *more* frigates, and a dozen destroyers, not to mention several dozen gunships."

"I have reasonable confidence one of those warships will not attack."

"Reasonable confidence? Exactly what does that mean?" Critch continued.

"Enough," Seda bellowed. "The *Arcadia* is in orbit, which means the fleet is focused on Heid at the moment. That may be what's preventing Ausyar from firing on another Terran target." He turned to Heid. "Have they tried to contact you yet?"

Her features smoothed, and she straightened. "They're broadcasting a message on endless loop. Corps General Ausyar demands the immediate surrender of my crew and me on the grounds of treason and theft of Collective property."

Which is true, Reyne thought to himself.

"Did he give you a time limit to respond?" Seda asked.

"No," she said. "He's stalling. After the frigates, I don't believe he's ready to initiate another attack until he better understands the *Arcadia*'s modifications. However, I'm keeping the entire crew on full alert. The moment they fire—either on us or on Terra—we will attack the *Unity*."

Seda placed his hands on his desk. "I believe we should use the *Arcadia* to our advantage. Now is the time to negotiate a peace treaty."

"We don't have the upper hand," Reyne said. "They'll take everything they can."

"They'll screw us on any negotiation," Critch agreed.

"You really think Ausyar will negotiate?" Heid asked.

"No," Seda said bluntly. "If I sit down with him, we'll know if Parliament is interested in peace, or how far they intend to go down the warpath. Sixx and I saw public opinion on Myr. Citizens are tired of feeding money into the CUF to monitor the colonies, most of which they don't even want. For every protest on Myr, there are dozens of protests taking place on Alluvia. The vast majority of Alluvians are even talking about breaking free from the Collective themselves. Public opinion is in our favor. Now is the perfect time to hold out our hands in peace. As the

Campaign drags on, citizens are bound to become apathetic, or worse, begin to side with the CUF."

Silence filled the room for a moment.

"I support negotiations," Reyne said. "We lost the first Uprising because the other side outlasted us. My greatest fear is to watch the same thing happen all over again."

"You have my support," Heid said. "As long as you stand firm and don't let them take rights away from the colonists. The colonies need to stand free. This may be our only chance to free them all."

"I'm in," Critch said. "If they try to screw us, we can use the blight."

Everyone turned to Critch.

"You didn't destroy that?" Reyne asked, slack-jawed.

Critch's lip curled upward.

Reyne guffawed. "We can't even think of using the blight. If we do, we're no better than them." He pointed to the sky, to where the fleet remained in orbit.

"Let's exhaust political options first," Seda said, sounding like a true diplomat. "If negotiations fail, then we must discuss how expansive the Campaign should become. I'm rich, but my accounts are draining fast. I cannot support a drawn-out war. Mason knows that, and will use any knowledge he can in his favor."

"We need to move headquarters," Critch said. "I don't like Mason knowing we're here."

"Mason knows we're here?" Reyne asked, tension coiling in his gut.

Seda opened and closed his artificial hand, as though disinterested in the conversation. "I suspect he knows."

"Then you need to relocate immediately," Heid said. "If Ausyar knew, he'd bomb you the first chance he got. If he were to kill you, the Campaign would be over."

"We're still here, which means Ausyar doesn't know. I think we have time. As we speak, I'm having supplies delivered to an asteroid inside the Space Coast. I had it staked out as a fallout shelter of sorts, and when I saw the direction the Collective was heading, I had the interior built out. I'd planned it to be a surprise for Mariner, so she did not know about it, which means Mason doesn't know about it. It can only support twenty people at this time, which works for us, but leaves our army out in the open. The Citadel provides some protection, but I don't like the idea of leaving our people behind to face the CUF's mercy."

"We've all seen firsthand the CUF doesn't know the term." Reyne swallowed. "Let's negotiate and finish this."

CHAPTER 14

PLAYING POLITICS

Rebus Station, Terra
Seda

FIVE HOURS ELAPSED before the official negotiation meeting. During that time, the torrent leaders hashed over the talking points, Seda notified the news of the event, and Ausyar would've consulted with Parliament—and, no doubt, Mason.

The meeting was held at the stationmaster's office in Rebus Station. Seda had offered to host, as it was customary for any political and business meeting of worth to take place on land.

Out of the three captains, Seda only permitted Critch to join him in the room. The other two marshals were furious to say the least, but Seda had been planning the Uprising for years, and he wasn't going to have Ausyar's personal conflicts get in the way of independence.

Ausyar considered Heid a Collective traitor, number one on the CUF's most-wanted list, and he'd have her shot on sight. She'd very publicly humiliated him. She was an officer promoted by him and entrusted with a warship, which she'd then stolen under his watch. He'd want to personally—and publicly—make her pay for her disrespect.

And Ausyar hated Reyne with the heat of a supernova, because Reyne had killed Ausyar's consort, Zara Wintsel. It didn't matter that Wintsel's death had been accidental, Ausyar single-mindedly sought to avenge her death. Seda suspected that Ausyar's pride had been stung worse than his heart at the loss of his consort.

Under Myrad law, Ausyar could satisfy his personal vendettas against Heid and Reyne without repercussions. That left Critch, aka Drake Fender, as the only torrent marshal who could be in the same room as Ausyar.

Ausyar had been chasing Critch for years, and it had to stick in Ausyar's craw that one man, basically a simple thief, had been able to evade the armada for so long. Critch and his specters had made more than one CUF commandant a laughing stock. Even now, during the Campaign, Critch drew volunteers by the hundreds, while Ausyar had to resort to drafting colonists to serve the Collective. Critch was a thorn in the corps general's side, plain and simple.

Seda rubbed his temples. Having Drake Fender—the scarred face of the torrent rebellion—in the room during negotiations would be crucial for the colonists to buy in to any peace treaty.

But hell. Torrent, pirate, whichever role Critch was playing that day, neither would contribute to good negotiations. Though, Seda had to give Critch credit. The man was an astute business-man, and a man Seda had come to respect. As a pirate, Critch had accumulated a fleet of over a dozen ships and countless prop-erties. But pirating was a far cry from politicking, even though both were cutthroat professions.

Seda read messages on his comm panel to keep anxiety from showing on his face. Critch lounged in a chair off to the side. He looked like he was napping, but Seda knew differently. *The pirate would make a damn good poker player*, Seda humored himself.

"Ausyar's arrived at the station," Hari said, and Seda looked up to see her at the doorway. She'd brought with her Tax and Corbin, Seda's two most trusted guards, and the trio placed themselves around the room where they could best protect Seda and watch for trouble.

Seda didn't really think there'd be an assassination attempt today, not with the meeting being recorded and sent out to all his news sources. Parliament would no doubt have the video clipped and modified to better tell their side of the story, but that would only benefit Seda, as Vapor would post the full, unedited video online for everyone to see.

He stood and moved to the center of the room, where two chairs had been set to establish an equal platform for the two leaders to speak. Out of habit, he checked his right side to make sure the robotic arm was firmly in place. He glanced over at Critch, to see the man's gaze now rapt on the door.

Two officers walked through the doorway and looked over the room. Seemingly satisfied, they turned and nodded. A commandant, who looked young for his position, walked in first, followed by Corps General Michel Ausyar, who was followed by four more officers. The corps general wore a blue uniform adorned with a chest full of pins and medals. Seda drily wondered how many of those Ausyar had actually earned and how many were for decoration.

The blue-hued Myrad looked across the faces in the room and seemed unimpressed. When his gaze settled on Seda, the general's nose lifted even higher in the air, a feat Seda hadn't thought possible.

"Corps General Ausyar, thank you for coming today." Seda gestured to the chairs. "Please, have a seat."

Ausyar chose a chair and gestured for Seda to sit, as though he were the host. "Mr. Faulk."

Seda didn't miss the fact that Ausyar hadn't used Seda's formal title of Stationmaster, and he knew the omission was an intentional power play. Ausyar was clearly trying to reduce Seda's status and, thereby, his power in negotiations. Seda wanted to laugh. The corps general thought he was the superior party in the room today. He had no idea.

Seda gracefully took a seat without comment or any betrayal of emotion. "We're here to discuss fair and equitable terms for a peace treaty."

Ausyar waved him off. "Let's cut to the chase, Mr. Faulk. The Collective authority of Myr and Alluvia established the colonies. They have been supported by the Collective and, in exchange, are expected to return support. I do not see any logic wherein they can make such inflammatory demands upon the Collective."

Seda continued as though he'd never been interrupted. "The first colony, right here where we're sitting today, was established 388 years ago. Since then, nearly a hundred colonies have been established on the four colony worlds—and in the Space Coast, if you were to count an asteroid belt. These colonies have grown and thrived, in part thanks to the Collective, and in part *despite* the Collective. Since the beginning of space travel, it's been universally accepted that all people are equal in every way. After all, we all originated from Earth. Yet here we are in a political predicament wherein people living in the colonies are being denied citizenship because they weren't born on either Alluvia or Myr. For nearly one hundred years, colonists have been asking for equal rights. Parliament has ignored those voices and has instead passed new legislation that further discriminate against the colonies in favor of bringing more money and power to Myr and Alluvia." Seda raised a finger. "Both of which were also considered colonies until they declared their independence and developed their own governance.

"Colonies either wilt or blossom. Those that bloom claim independence. That is the natural evolution for every colony. We only need to look at Mars and Europa for examples, and Earth's country nations before that. The fringe has reached the point where independence is as necessary as air for the colonies to survive and thrive. We've made our intentions clear and desire no war, but legalized discrimination and undue taxation must end now. All the colonies must be free. Only then will humanity thrive across the stars."

Ausyar sighed and blinked heavily as if Seda had nearly put him to sleep. "Mr. Faulk, you talk of the colonies as being separate from the Collective, but all six planets constitute the Collective. Every planet is a contributor to the Collective's success. We value the colony worlds as much as we value the citizen worlds."

"I must disagree," Seda said. "If all six planets are equal parts of the whole, why are the colonies taxed at *thirty-six* times the tax rate charged to citizens of Alluvia and Myr? Why, then, is there only one senator to represent four colony worlds in Parliament, while Alluvia and Myr each have five delegates? In a democratic Parliament, a ratio such as that only guarantees the colonies have no voice."

Ausyar shrugged. "Parliament was established before the colonies were founded. Delegation was based on population size. Of course, Myr and Alluvia have more delegates."

"If delegates align with population size, then why hasn't the Parliament structure changed in over three hundred years? Colonists outnumber citizens three to one. By your logic, if Parliament were a democratic structure, the fringe would send thirty delegates, not one. To me, it seems Parliament is hamstringing the voice of the colonies."

Impatience darkened Ausyar's face. "Did you ask me here

today so you could lecture me on the Collective government structure, or do you have a point to make? I'm a busy man, Mr. Faulk, and have little time for a tête-à-tête."

Seda smiled inwardly, and he imagined Critch was finding similar humor in watching Ausyar's annoyance swell. "I'm here to discuss with you the terms of removing all colony planets from the Collective."

Ausyar raised his brows. "And am I to understand you have the authority to speak for all colonies?"

"I do," Seda replied with confidence. "Representatives of every fringe station have given me authority to represent their planet's interests."

"Parliament speaks for the colonies, not you."

"Wrong. Per the declaration of independent fringe colonies, we no longer recognize Parliament's authority as a governing structure." Seda flipped it back to Ausyar. "And I suppose you have the license to speak for the Collective?"

"I'm here under the authority of the Collective Unified Forces."

"Does that authority include Parliament and the Collective overall?"

Ausyar shifted in his chair. "Of course."

Seda could've stopped the conversation then and there. At that moment, he knew Ausyar did not have Parliament's full backing. If Parliament didn't agree with the treaty—or any parts thereof—that Ausyar negotiated, they'd conjure a legal loophole to make the treaty null and void.

Still, Seda chose to continue the meeting. He leaned back in his chair before speaking. "The Fringe Liberation Campaign as well as the Rebus Reclamation Effort is the direct result of the colonies demanding independence. I feel I can speak for both of us when I say we do not want a physical conflict, and we all desire peace."

"Peace?" Ausyar chortled. "You talk of peace, yet you burned down every fuel production plant on Terra. That doesn't sound like peace to me."

Seda shrugged. "They were my production facilities. As full owner, I may choose what to do with each of my facilities. I chose to remove fuel for space travel from the current equation. I broke no law in closing them down, and no one was harmed."

"I wonder if the Terrans would agree with your statement. After all, you took away the livelihoods of thousands of colonists just to make a statement"

"Perhaps. However, I think you'll find colonists are quite resilient," Seda said. "I wonder if the Collective economy can show the same resilience."

Ausyar's eyes narrowed, and Seda noticed the older man's knuckles were whitening.

Now.

"Does the Collective want peace, Corps General?" Seda asked.

Ausyar seemed surprised by the question. "Of course."

"Then, what terms do you propose?"

Ausyar straightened in his chair. "We are prepared to offer Playa and the Space Coast independence after a transition stage, in return for an immediate cease-fire on all other colony planets."

Seda laughed for effect. He found, in fact, the proposal to be downright contemptible and not the least bit funny. "The Space Coast is already a neutral colony and has never had any ties, let alone an arrangement, with the Collective."

Ausyar raised a finger. "However, the asteroid belt falls within Collective space. Therefore, Parliament may elect to incorporate it into the overall Collective at any point."

Seda gave Ausyar an incredulous look. "We both know that the Space Coast offers no value in the eyes of the Collective. With minimal metals to mine, that asteroid belt is nothing more than a bunch of rocks. And Playa..." Seda exhaled deeply. "Well, you've already bombed the largest colony and only fringe station on that planet, which doesn't leave a lot for survivors."

Ausyar raised his brows. "If that offer is not sufficient, tell me what you propose."

Seda leaned forward and eyed the corps general like a hawk zeroing in on prey. "Parliament will recognize full independence of *all* four colony planets. In return, we offer open trade with the Collective with trade treaties to be established separately by each fringe station."

Ausyar sneered. "The colonies can't simply claim independence and have it happen. Parliament may consider Playa and Spate as candidates for independence, but Terra and Darios will remain within Collective control."

Seda gave a humorless grin. "Ah, yes. Terra and Darios would remain under Collective *control*. No, Corps General, I'm afraid that is not acceptable. We have already declared independence for all colonies. The four planets beyond Myr and Alluvia will stand as their own. That truth is unequivocal and cannot be denied. We will *not* leave any of our brethren under your *control*."

Seda abruptly stood, knowing the small action would be seen as an affront to Ausyar, and sure enough, the corps general's eyes widened at the slight. The man huffed.

Seda ignored him. "I believe we've reached an impasse. Unless you can offer a solution that recognizes every colony world as an independent world, with no Collective oversight, then the Fringe Liberation Campaign will continue. Going forward, the lives lost as a result of your inability to negotiate fall upon your and the Collective's shoulders."

Ausyar jumped to his feet. "You are talking to the Corps General of the Collective Unified Forces. Show respect, colonist!"

At that moment, Seda knew he'd hit publicity gold in winning colonists' hearts to the cause, and he had to focus to not betray any sense of success in his expression. Not that the infuriated Ausyar noticed. The Myrad's egotism didn't allow him to see his own faux pas.

Ausyar fumed. "Your little declaration isn't recognized by Parliament, and certainly not by me. The colonies remain under Collective control and must abide by Collective law immediately. You also must turn over Aramis Reyne for the murder of Dr. Zara Wintsel, a citizen, and turn over Gabriela Heid and her entire crew for treason. In addition, you will return the *Arcadia* and the *Matador,* both of which are stolen property of the Collective Unified Forces. If you do not cease and desist these attacks against citizens immediately, all colonists will be treated as terrorists to the Collective, and I will crush you all, starting with you." He pointed at Seda's chest.

Hook, line, and sinker. Seda wanted to smile. Instead, he grimaced. "I see that we cannot have an objective discussion, and so I believe we're done here."

He motioned for Ausyar to leave.

Ausyar wagged his finger at Seda. "Watch yourself. You think that because you have made some money, you have some kind of power. But you can't buy your way to citizenship. You're a colonist, and you'll die a colonist. You are foolish to think you have any say whatsoever. You're nothing but a cockroach, Faulk, and I look forward to silencing you once and for all."

Seda said nothing.

Ausyar left the room with a swagger Seda had seen only Myrads pull off. The moment Ausyar's envoy departed, Seda walked to his desk and turned off the recording. Hari closed and locked the door.

He turned to Hari and Critch. "That was rather interesting."

"You were right," Hari said. "Parliament has no interest in negotiating."

Critch smiled. "I didn't realize a Myrad could turn so blue."

Seda leaned back onto his desk. "We know the truth now. Ausyar pulled out of Rebus Station to attack rather than to discuss peace. I believe he's planning to cripple Terra like he did Playa by bombing the space docks." He turned to Critch. "I support our plan to attack first. Tell the *Arcadia* to jump."

CHAPTER 15

SMOKE AND MIRRORS

Nova Colony, Space Coast
Heid

HEID HAD NEVER THOUGHT she'd fly the *Arcadia* through the Space Coast again. This time, Will had graciously relinquished the controls before they'd even entered the Coast. She navigated the warship through the asteroid belt, adding a few more dings and scrapes to the warship.

She imagined Ausyar had ranted for some time when the *Arcadia* had gone into jump speed within visual distance of the fleet, leaving them wondering what she was up to. *Good.*

She never left the ship when they reached Nova Colony, which was back up and running, thanks to Stan. The *Arcadia's* transport ships were busy making runs between the warship and the colony, bringing crewmembers and supplies to the asteroid. It'd taken nearly two days—far too long in Heid's opinion—to strip everything of value from the warship. When all of it, including all transport ships and gunships, had been moved to

Nova Colony, she felt like a weight had been lifted from her shoulders. If only she could fly the *Arcadia* alone.

"They'll be safe at Nova Colony," Sylvian said.

Heid looked up to see her crewmember watching her with concern. "I know. It's you and everyone stuck on board with me that I worry about."

Sylvian chuckled. "There're only twelve of us left. When you walk through the hallways, they *echo*." When Heid didn't smile, she continued. "We volunteered for this mission. You didn't force any of us into this."

"Jump coordinates are programmed," Nolin announced from the navigator's seat. "We're ready to jump the moment we're clear of the Coast."

Heid straightened. "Then, let's get going."

Stress added to her reaction time, and the return trip through the asteroid belt was not some of her best flying. In a way, she was fortunate there weren't too many crewmembers on board to rib her about it later. As she cleared the final asteroid, Nolin sent the warship into jump speed. It would take seven jumps to cover over four hundred quadrants between the Space Coast and Terra, since there was no straight path from their current coordinates.

Traveling through jump speed was as smooth as flying off solar power, even though the ship was traveling at point-three light speed. She used the time to prepare the escape pods, working alongside the crew not busy monitoring the jump systems and engines.

She cringed, looking at the escape pods, small tubes that lined the ship's hull. They were every dromadier's worst nightmare. Escape pods had minimal life support systems, and nothing else. They were essentially logs that would travel in whichever direction they were jettisoned, and survivors would pray they'd be found before they died a miserably slow death in space. She triple-checked that the pods' beacons were set to the encrypted channel Critch would be monitoring.

Each tube would hold three people stuffed in it as tightly as a fresh recruit's duffel bag. With a skeleton crew of twelve, they needed only four pods. While at Nova Colony, she'd had those pods painted flat black so they wouldn't reflect any light. The metal in them could still be picked up on radar, but she'd figured there would be enough debris to hide within—as long as shrapnel didn't slice through them first.

By the time they started their fifth jump, they were a couple million clicks from Darios, and Heid could see the beautiful world through her viewing panel. It was a bittersweet sight. That was the colony that would make or break any peace treaty. She knew the Collective would never give up the garden world, but the remaining colonies needed Darion food for survival.

The Collective. Her fingers trembled as she contemplated making the call to Barrett. If the others knew she was telling him the plan, they'd think she was crazy. She'd been betrayed by someone she cared for before, but she told herself that if she became jaded and no longer had faith in anyone, she'd become like her father. Even though it terrified her to do so, she made the call.

When she hung up, she let out a breath and relaxed. Whatever Barrett did next was up to him. Would he betray her, or would he help?

She glanced at her hand to see it no longer shaking, and she realized now that control was out of her ability, the stress had become dampened.

After the sixth jump, Heid had Nolin and the crew take a break. She spent the time catching up on the news, as it couldn't be obtained during jumps.

No surprise, Parliament had never reached out to Seda to counter Ausyar's terms. Vapor had loaded the full video onto the network, yet Parliament had remained quiet. The networks were filled with chatter comparing the differences between the full fourteen-minute video and the forty-second video the DZ-Five News broadcast. The edited video covered Ausyar offering terms, and Seda standing and saying, *"I think we're done here."*

She shook her head and scrolled through other articles. Her fingers froze on a headline several pages down.

LINA TAO PUBLICLY EXECUTED FOR TREASON
DZ-Five News Reporter Found Guilty of Conspiring Against Citizen Welfare

---

Heid's temper roiled as she read the article. Lina had been her best friend through grade school and her roommate at the academy. She had no doubt her father had made sure Lina faced a firing squad simply to make a point—*I can take everything from you.*

Her jaw tightened. She looked forward to showing him she was her father's daughter. She would make sure he paid for all his crimes, and paid for them with his life.

Her door chimed, and Sylvian stepped in. "Nolin is ready for jump seven."

Heid felt steel in her bones. "I'm ready."

She watched the countdown. The hours ticked by interminably slowly. When they had two hours to go, she put the ship on alert status and made sure everyone knew exactly what they needed to do the moment they came out of jump speed.

When the moment came, a visual of the fleet—with the *Unity* in dead center—filled the wall screen. Heid gripped her captain's chair. "Raise shields. Arm phase cannons."

"Aye, aye, Captain," Sylvian obliged.

"Now, *run!*" Heid yelled.

Heid, Nolin, and Sylvian ran off the bridge. They sprinted—God, it felt like they were so slow—down the never-ending corridor until they reached their designated escape pod. She prayed the three other pods were already loaded and ready to go.

Heid pressed Nolin and then Sylvian into their stations, where five-point harness held each in a standing position. As soon as both were secure, she squeezed in and set her harness. The door closed, enveloping them in total darkness. She counted to five, then hit the release button.

The pod jettisoned down with such force that all three people inside grunted. She was sure her collarbone was broken, if not badly bruised. The pod suddenly changed direction again, this time brutally, at a right angle. *Too late!* Heid's head hit something, and all sensation blinked away into single flash of light.

CHAPTER 16

JUST DESERTS

In orbit above Rebus Station, Terra
Critch

THE *HONORLESS* EASED in behind the *Unity* with the systems turned down to minimal support and no engine power. The pirate ship, painted a flat black and in stealth mode, would be nearly impossible to see by anyone not searching specifically for it. If the *Arcadia* didn't arrive soon, he'd have to use a nav engine to keep from running up into the *Unity*'s tailpipes.

Birk jogged onto the bridge.

Critch looked him over. "Is it done?"

Birk grinned and held up a black marker. "It's done."

"Good. Buckle in."

They waited. Critch's adrenaline-soaked muscles began to throb as they waited. But he didn't stand. He knew he'd have only seconds to react when the *Arcadia* arrived. It took forty more minutes of waiting before the *Arcadia* blinked into view. Light glows straightaway surrounded the CUF ships.

"Their shields are up," Birk said. "She's got their full attention."

"Wait for it," Critch drawled. Ships vibrated as their phase cannons lit up. One shot, followed by more. "Now!"

In the middle of the phase blast lightshow, the *Honorless* fired off a single, unarmed torpedo. It had no systems and no metal, so scans couldn't pick it up. Critch's ship was close enough, he watched the torpedo fly unscathed through the energy shields and lodge itself into the *Unity*'s hull.

Critch zoomed in the viewing panel to make sure the torpedo had broken all the way through the hull.

"Oh, yeah." Birk grinned. "It breached for sure."

Critch nodded as he looked at the torpedo. Only its tail remained outside. The rest of it had broken through. He held up his finger for a brief second before tapping it on the button that would cause the torpedo to burst open. They'd removed all explosives from the device, so it would display on the *Unity*'s systems as a minimal breach. By the time they sent techs down to repair the hull, it would be too late.

A flash of light caused him to wince. He looked to see the *Arcadia* was gone. The black vacuum of space smothered flames from the exploding ship. Left in the warship's place was a sea of debris, flying outward. Ever since he was a kid, he'd found it a bit unnerving there was no sound in space. Plenty to see, but nothing to hear. He used to blast classical music to fill the void. Now, he had it play softly in the background.

He entered the frequency for the escape pods and noticed four pod beacons online. He was relieved to see they'd ejected in time. "Now, let's go get our girl before the fleet discovers her."

Sneaking up behind the *Unity* had been nerve-wracking. Flying around the fleet and through shooting debris while in stealth mode was damn near the riskiest thing Critch had ever done. Well, that, and searching for survivors in a minefield. Then, he'd been so careful to avoid mines that he'd never even considered a dead soldier could be gripping a grenade without its pin. With the explosion's damage to his upper body, Critch had felt—and looked—like ground meat for months.

People often asked him why he didn't have surgery to remove the scars. They had no idea he needed those scars—when he looked in the mirror every day, the scars reminded him of everything he'd done and everyone he'd killed. He'd never be able to erase those memories and so erasing the physical scars felt like a lie.

Critch had chosen to pilot the *Honorless* on this mission. Gabe was a good pilot, but Critch was the best. If the fleet detected them, they'd be dead, plain and simple. It'd be impossible to escape an entire fleet of ships that had their cannons already armed, targeted in their direction.

"Birk, I need you to monitor every ship of that fleet," Critch ordered. "Let me know if even a patrol ship sneezes."

"I'm on it, Boss."

Critch flew the pirate ship—a highly-modified yacht—slowly around the fleet, using the nav engines on their lowest settings to minimize their moisture trail. Stealth made a ship invisible to scanners, nothing more. The key to not being seen was the flat black paint that didn't reflect anything. Even then, if someone happened to be looking in the right direction, they could notice the temporary disappearance of a star as the *Honorless* passed between.

On today's mission, the likelihood of being seen was much higher, as every CUF ship over Rebus Station had eyes on the debris, shooting at any remaining chunks of the warship with a trajectory heading toward the fleet. Worse, if any shrapnel was headed for the *Honorless*, he couldn't shoot it without giving away his position. He'd reinforced the rilon hull, but a big enough chunk of metal could destroy his ship.

Critch respected Gabriela Heid, liked her even, but if it came down to choosing the safety of his crew or the escape pods, he'd leave the pods to the abyss. He rubbed his prickly jaw. It was exactly that kind of thinking that made him deserve the scars he bore.

"I have ship movement," Birk said.

"Did they see us?"

"Hold on. No, it looks like two patrol ships are making their way to the *Unity*. I'm guessing someone is wondering why the *Unity* went silent."

It took over an hour to navigate around the fleet, keeping a wide berth. During that time, the fleet stayed in position, though Critch wondered how much chatter was taking place in regard to the *Unity*.

The *Arcadia* had expanded to cover an area of several thousand clicks. If the pods didn't have beacons, he'd never find them. As it was, two pods had jettisoned off the warship at roughly the same time and velocity and in the same direction, keeping them within a hundred click radius. The other two were several thousand clicks apart, and splitting farther every minute.

All four beacons were identical, so he had no way of knowing which pod Heid was in. That meant he had to pick them up as he found them, placing no pod as a higher priority. He chose to pick up the pair of pods first.

They drew nearer to the first pod, and Critch sucked in a breath through clenched teeth. "That's not good," he said.

Birk looked up from his panel and whistled. "I sure hope the others are in better shape."

Critch didn't even bother getting any closer. The pod had been cleanly cut in half by a sheet of the *Arcadia*'s hull, which had lodged in one of the halves. Streaks of blood marred the hull. The three crewmembers on board never stood a chance.

The second pod was within ten clicks of the first one, which was surprising given the massive force of the explosion. This one had a big dent, but Critch couldn't make out if the pod had been breached.

Critch opened the ship's internal comms. "Nat, Burl, prepare for one pod retrieval. We've got one ready for pickup."

"We're at our stations now," Nat responded.

Critch brought the ship up alongside the escape pod. From the side viewing panel, he could see Nate extend the ship's crane and close the claw around the pod. The crane bent around to slide the pod inside the open freight door, which Burl operated, though Critch didn't bother checking the ship's internal monitors.

When the freight door closed, Critch received a comm via Burl's space suit. "Pod is secure. Do you want me to refresh the air and open the pod?"

"No," Critch replied. "Wait to air the bay until we've retrieved all the pods. They have air. They can wait until we land."

They switched direction and headed off for the nearest pod. Debris slammed into the hull, and Critch ducked. "Where did that come from?"

Birk flipped through his scans. "The fleet's breaking up the larger debris, likely hoping they can send some of the bigger chunks to burn up in the atmosphere."

"They're sucking at it," Critch grumbled. "They're turning Terra's orbit into a junkyard, that's what they're doing." He sighed and refocused on the third pod.

Critch sped up slightly to get to it. He knew he was pushing his luck flying around a debris zone with the fleet within shooting distance. The third pod was in a congested mess of debris. It was scratched, but looked in surprisingly good shape.

He grimaced. He didn't like the idea of extending the crane into that clutter, and the thought crossed his mind to leave the pod. Instead, he tapped the internal comms. "Nat, Burl, prepare for one pod retrieval. We've got another one ready for pickup."

"We're ready to go," Nat replied.

As Critch neared the debris, small chunks bounced off the ship. He winced at every thump and vibration. He watched the crane extend. Debris knocked it around. When what looked like a bunk hit it, he thought the crane was going to snap, but it held. It looked like Nat sped the crane up to move things along faster. The moment the crane had the pod, it zoomed back to the ship.

Three minutes later, Burl's voice reported, "Pod is secure."

"Good," Critch said and immediately banked to head off for the fourth and final pod. It was the farthest from the fleet, which was why he'd left it for last, knowing it would be the easiest to retrieve. It took longer than expected to catch up to it, as it was moving at a good clip.

When they reached it, there was no debris in the vicinity, making it an easy catch. The pod looked in perfect condition. "Nat, Burl, prepare for one pod retrieval."

The pod slowly spun as it flew. When it spun around halfway, Critch frowned. "No, cancel that. No more pod pickups."

The pod door was missing. The locks had likely failed upon jettison. Critch could make out two frozen bodies inside. The third body would have been strapped to the door, and was likely hundreds of clicks away by now.

"Brr," Birk said. "That's why you'll never get me into one of those banana peels."

"No kidding," Critch said in agreement, and tapped the comms. "Everyone to your stations. We're heading to Terra."

The *Honorless* made faster time back to the planet, since Critch could steer farther from the fleet.

As they approached Terra's orbit, Critch began to program landing sequences for Seda's spaceport.

"Whoa, we have *major* movement going on right now," Birk said.

Critch tensed. "What's happening?"

"The fleet's leaving orbit. I mean, the *Unity*'s not moving, of course, but the rest of them are following the second warship."

Critch considered for a moment. "Who's the commandant on the second warship?"

"No idea. Whoever it is doesn't seem to have much interest in breathing down Terra's neck."

"We'll take what we can get," Critch said, and then broke through the atmosphere.

After the *Honorless* landed, Critch headed back to the cargo hold, where Burl was opening the pods.

Critch felt relief when he saw Heid's long dark hair as she crawled out of one. He strode over and helped her to her feet. "How's it feel to be dead?"

She touched her forehead and winced. "It hurts more than I expected."

He reached forward and lightly touched the swollen, red area. "That's some bump. I'd bet you've got a concussion. But you could've gotten worse. You saved your crew's lives by giving up the *Arcadia*."

She seemed pleased, and then glanced over at the pods. The five other crewmembers they'd retrieved seemed conscious and well. She frowned. "There are only two pods."

He swallowed. "Two pods were breached."

"No." She closed her eyes and turned away.

"Losing six lives instead of hundreds should be counted as a win," Critch said.

She sighed. "Losing good people is *always* a loss." A thought seemed to hit her, and she turned abruptly to Critch. "And Ausyar?"

"A life that won't be missed," he replied.

She nodded. "But I still feel for all the other lives on the *Unity*."

"I know," he replied and felt a small pang that he didn't share the same feeling.

When Burl opened the freight door, Critch helped Heid walk down the ramp.

"By the way," he began. "The fleet's broken orbit. They've established out by the moon."

"Oh?" Heid seemed surprised at first, then pleased.

"I take it you have a friend on that warship?"

Her smile spread. "I think so."

CHAPTER 17

AN UNEXPECTED GIFT

REYNE RUSHED DOWN the dock the moment the door to the *Honorless* opened.

When he saw Critch assisting Heid down the ramp, relief flooded him. She'd survived. The crazy, harebrained idea of faking her and her crew's deaths by letting Ausyar destroy the *Arcadia* had worked. The Campaign had lost its greatest asset, but at the same time had secured the safety of over three hundred lives.

He walked over to greet them. When he reached them, he embraced Heid. She immediately tensed as if she hadn't ever been hugged, but then wrapped an arm around him. He took a step back. "You pulled it off. I never thought I'd say it, but I think you're crazier than Critch here."

She grinned. "It definitely was easier in theory than in practice."

He grew concerned. "Your crew that flew with you on this mission?"

She winced. "We lost six."

He closed his eyes and lowered his head for a brief moment. "The eversea has gained six brave souls." While six was a low number for such a high-risk mission, he would've been happier if there'd been no deaths. He turned to Critch. "And your crew?"

"Without a scratch," Critch replied.

He exhaled a sigh. "Good. Today, we had a major win against the CUF, thanks to you and your crew." When neither spoke, Reyne motioned. "Come. Seda wants to meet Gabriela."

The trio headed to the hangar to find Seda working at his desk.

Heid cocked her head. "I honestly never thought I'd meet the Aeronaut."

Seda came to his feet and held out his arm. "Welcome, Baker. However, I believe you go by your real name now you're no longer associated with the Founders."

She clasped his forearm in salutation. "It's a pleasure, Seda."

He nodded toward her injury. "You should get that looked at."

"I will," she said and took a seat.

Critch walked over to the bar and poured himself a whiskey. He downed the glass and refilled it.

Seda watched Critch. "Did everything go as planned?"

Critch nodded. "Exactly as planned."

"Except we lost two escape pods," Heid added.

Seda frowned. "I'm sorry to hear that. I'm sure they were good people."

"The best," Heid said.

A chime sounded. Seda opened the drawer and pulled out a tablet that only a few people in the Collective knew about. "I don't believe it," he said. "It's Mason."

Shivers coursed over Reyne. He strode over, closed the door, and then leaned against the wall.

Seda furrowed his brows. "What is he up to?" He shook off the expression. "Let's find out, shall we?"

Seda transferred the call to the wall screen, and Mason—also known as Gabriel Heid—appeared. While everyone in the room could see and hear Mason, Mason could only see Seda.

"Hello, Aeronaut," Mason said.

"Mason," Seda said, following suit. "To what do I owe this call today?"

"First things first. How's my daughter?"

Seda kept his poker face. "I'm afraid Corps General Ausyar launched an attack against the *Arcadia* earlier today. All souls aboard, including your daughter, were killed."

Mason pursed his lips. "I saw the footage, and I applaud the subterfuge. However, I know Gabriela loved that ship. And I know the only thing she loved more than that ship was her crew. I knew she had something up her sleeve when she jumped from orbit."

"She's gone," Seda reiterated. "But I don't understand why you'd care. Wasn't it just last year you tried to capture her on Spate?"

Mason gave a small smile. "Capture, not *kill*, Aeronaut. Gabriela is still my daughter and the only family I have left. Of course I care about her well-being."

Reyne shot a glance at Heid, to see her roll her eyes, and he was glad she had the common sense to remain silent.

"I suspect you care about your daughter's well-being about as much as you cared about Mariner's well-being when you tortured her to death," Seda said.

Mason cocked his head. "You're still bothered about that little incident?"

"She was my wife." Seda nearly spat the words.

Mason sobered. "Then you shouldn't have digressed from our plans."

"*Your* plans," Seda corrected, glaring. "They were never the Founders' plans."

Mason waved a hand through the air. "What's done is done. Now, I hope you will convey to my daughter that she's in my thoughts," Mason continued.

"Why did you call?" Seda asked.

"I'm calling about what you did today, of course. I must say, I was quite impressed to hear you had the courage to kill Corps General Ausyar, though I thought writing 'Broken Mountain' on the torpedo was rather melodramatic. You could've handled it in a different way than making it look like terrorism."

Reyne stiffened, confused. What torpedo? Ausyar was dead? When the words on the torpedo sunk in, he spun to face Critch. Critch sat in his chair, with a glass of whiskey in one hand, watching Reyne. He didn't look the least bit bothered. If anything, the bastard looked smug. Reyne shot him a dark look and then turned away. *I'll deal with you later.*

"I see you're still closely connected with your sources in the CUF," Seda said. "What else did they tell you?"

"That the blight you released on the *Unity* killed all 455 souls on board, as well as eighteen souls on board the two patrol ships sent to investigate."

The blight. Reyne's jaw slackened, and he forced himself to breathe slowly and deeply to keep from attacking Critch at that precise moment.

"Parliament is worried. They're afraid this was a warning shot, and your next target is them." Mason shrugged. "I encourage that perception."

Seda's gaze narrowed. "Why is that?"

"Because I want the colonies to be free. Or, at least, to believe they're free. That way, they get this little rebellious streak out of their systems and they realize they can't last on their own without support. How long do you give the colonies before they come back to Parliament with their tails between their legs, begging to be brought back into the Collective?"

Seda laughed. "You never understood the mind of a colonist."

"And you've never understood the difference between a revolution and a civil war. The colonies needed to experience a revolution, but you never needed to take them into war."

"I've done and will continue to do whatever is needed to ensure the colonies are free. If you remember, Mason, the original purpose of the Founders was to ensure equality and independence."

"The colonies didn't even exist when the Founders met for the first time," Mason said.

"I remember the greatest thing the Founders ever accomplished was to instigate civil war between Myr and Alluvia."

Mason's brows rose. "And I suppose you're likening yourself to the original Founders. Aeronaut, you're no Jacob Mason."

"Nor do I pretend to be." Seda gave a sly smile. "After all, I'm not the one who took the first Founder's name upon initiation."

"Enough chitchat," Mason said. "The first reason I called is to congratulate you on taking care of Ausyar for me. I especially like the irony of him dying by his own creation."

"Hm. Now, I suspect you're playing me. I know you steered his empiric motivations. He never would've had the blight without your guidance."

"Ah, Ausyar proved to be a disappointment. He had the ambition and resources to unify the Collective. But he also had greed. And that weakness tends to make one shortsighted."

"You only want to rule the entire Collective," Seda sneered. "I suppose that's not greed?"

Mason narrowed his gaze before he brushed the air with his hand. "Now, to the second reason I called. I know my daughter is there with you, so what I have to say now is for her. Gabriela, you made a mistake to come to Terra. You should have stayed on Playa where you were safe. Now you've lost the *Arcadia*, which will cripple your little rebellion, even if you don't see it yet."

Reyne watched Heid's features tighten as she listened, and he was surprised she didn't speak up.

"Without the *Arcadia*, you are effectively defenseless," Mason continued. "And so, I wish to help you. I am sending you a file; what you do with it is up to you. The file is secure with your DNA—no one else can open it. If you choose to use it, it will give the Fringe Liberation Campaign what it needs to turn Parliament's opinion to its favor. In this file, you'll find all the proof you need that the creation and subsequent use of that terrible blight was done under Corps General Michel Ausyar's orders, and that he had desires to take over the Collective. Use this file, and you'll be safe from the CUF because the conflict will be over." Mason paused. "I know we've had our differences of late, but as I told Aeronaut, you are still my daughter even if you no longer adhere to the Founders code. I want you to be safe."

When Mason didn't say anything else, Seda spoke. "Is that all?"

Mason straightened, then gave a half-nod.

"For the free," Seda said.

Mason hung up.

Heid jumped to her feet. "What a conceited, pompous, arrogant ass!"

"Do you believe anything he said?" Critch asked her.

"No," she said quickly, paused for a moment, then shook her head. "No, I don't. He doesn't do anything that wouldn't help his cause. Helping *me* certainly doesn't accomplish that."

"What do you want done with the file?" Seda asked. "I can delete it if you wish."

Heid thought for a long moment. "I'll have Vapor check it out first. If it's clean, I'll take a look and see if it's what he says it is."

Seda nodded. "If it is, it would be a PR miracle."

Reyne pushed off from the wall and looked across the three faces in the room. "You were all in on it."

They turned to face him.

"You knew I was against using the blight. You had a meeting *after* our meeting to plan the *Arcadia* mission."

"You made it clear you wouldn't support the idea," Seda said.

"Of course I wouldn't!" Reyne yelled. "You saw what the blight did to Sol Base. We're now as guilty as Ausyar."

"We had to stop Ausyar," Seda said. "He bombed Broken Mountain. He was about to bomb Rebus Station, and then work his way through the colonies."

Reyne shook his head. "You didn't have to kill five hundred people to kill one man."

"That was my idea," Heid said quietly.

Reyne snapped on her. "Is that what the CUF taught you? To kill one person, take out a city?"

"No," she said. "It's what my father taught me. If we'd killed only Ausyar, Parliament would wonder what we're capable of. By using the blight to kill Ausyar, Parliament would tremble at what we're capable of. Now, they'll be willing to negotiate."

"And you can fly off into the stars," Reyne finished, then sighed. "Your impatience has cost us our honor." He rubbed his forehead and turned away from the group.

"What's done is done," Seda said. "Reyne, I realize now that you should have been there. You have my word that all major decisions going forward must be discussed and voted on by all three marshals. You, Critch, and Gabriela are a triad, each with your own strengths. You balance out one another. The colonies need each of you to fight for their freedom."

As Seda spoke, a decision came to Reyne. He felt the arthritis in his joints, he felt the sorrow of losing Throttle, and he felt the anguish Sixx was going through. He knew where he needed to be. He turned back to face them. "As leaders, it's our job to represent the best of the colonists. What happened today was the opposite. We showed the entire Collective we're no different than Ausyar when we want something. You've taken the Campaign down a path I never would've gone, and now you need to ride it where it leads. I can't be a part of that."

With that, he opened the door and left.

He'd made it halfway through the hangar before he heard footsteps behind him. He turned, surprised to see Critch was the one to come after him.

Reyne sighed. "I know you fired the torpedo. Did it take away the pain of losing Broken Mountain?"

Critch shook his head. "No. But I couldn't sit by and watch Ausyar bomb the next Broken Mountain. Not when there was something I could do about it."

"I know," Reyne said. "I don't blame you for wanting revenge, but you shouldn't have cut me out. We could've found another way."

"This was the only way," Critch said.

"There's *always* another way." Reyne turned, then took a deep sigh. "I know your intentions are good, but that doesn't change the fact you crossed a line when you used the blight. You should've destroyed it the moment you saw it. Instead, you used it to make a statement, no different than how Ausyar used it. There's nothing I can do for the Campaign, but I can look after my crew. So that's exactly what I'm going to do."

Reyne started walking.

"I hope you find her," Critch said.

Reyne paused for a moment, and then kept on walking.

CHAPTER 18

DATA DUMP

HEID SAT at the desk in her room at Seda's retreat and reread the message from Vapor for the umpteenth time.

Data file is clean. No risks detected.

She blew out a breath and leaned back. She never expected she'd be sitting there, deciding whether to open the file or not. She'd assumed the file was dirty, with a Trojan, virus, or something else. _But the best hacker in the Collective verified it's clean, so it has to be clean, right?_

She tentatively placed her hand on the scanner. After the system accepted her DNA as a match, it took several seconds to open the file. She began to have second thoughts, when it finally opened. A recording of her father started playing. She frowned.

Hello, Gabriela. I'm glad you opened this file. I wish we could have spoken again, but I suppose that's not possible, since my daughter died the day she betrayed me, the Founders, and the Collective.

Heid's eyes grew wide, and she tried to shut off the playback, but it wouldn't stop.

Today, the person who continues to bear the name Gabriela Heid will cease to exist so that my daughter may rest in peace. Goodbye Gabriela.

She jumped to her feet at the same time the computer exploded with the force of a small bomb.

Gabriela Heid never felt a thing.

CHAPTER 19

FINDING THE EVERSEA

Torrent Headquarters, Terra
Reyne

THE *GRYPHON* WASN'T SCHEDULED to depart until the next morning, which meant Reyne had to stay another night at Seda's retreat. He had just settled in bed to read, when the lights flickered, followed by an explosion that shook the walls. He dashed out into the hallway to see Critch, wearing only pants, jump out from his room. They caught each other's eyes for an instant before turning to see smoke curl out from under Heid's door.

"No." The word spilt from Reyne's slack-jawed lips.

The pair raced down the hallway to her room.

Critch reached the door first and tried to open it. "Locked," he growled and pounded on the door. "Heid!"

Seda came running down the hallway. "Move." He shoved Critch to the side and placed his hand over the access screen. The lock clicked, and Seda threw the door open.

The building's air system was already sucking out the smoky

air, leaving behind the stench of burnt wires. Computer shards were impaled in the walls. The three men rushed into the room to find Heid crumpled on the floor.

Seda reached her first. He kneeled and tenderly rolled her over. He didn't check for a pulse. It was obvious that he didn't need to. The computer had exploded with such force that hundreds of small pieces had hit her chest like a shotgun blast at short range. The front of her body was darkened by electrical soot and blood.

He wiped a tuft of hair from Heid's face. Critch and Reyne stood next to him, looking down at her.

Hari squeezed between Critch and Reyne. She fell to her knees next to Seda. She clenched her fists against her mouth. "*No.*"

Reyne looked over to where the computer had sat. There was nothing left except char where even the metal had melted in places. The power supply was a black hole. He thought back to the lights in his room. The code had somehow suppressed any electrical system safeguards while calling a power surge at such speed and intensity as to create a single burst of energy.

It was a genius, horrific plan. He grimaced, unable to fathom what Mason had done. How could a man kill his own daughter?

He swallowed back the bile coming into his mouth. "The data file. Mason included a kill code with the file."

"Mason," Critch snarled, and began pacing the room with clenched fists. "I should've killed him back on Alluvia."

"Impossible. Heid had Vapor scan the file," Seda said, stiffened, and then growled, "Vapor was the one who embedded the code in the first place."

Hari leaned on the floor for support. "I don't understand why a hacker would do this. She's helped us on several occasions."

Seda scowled. "She helped because we paid her well. She's

known throughout the fringe as the best hacker out there. Mason would know her, and I imagine he paid even better."

In a fury, Critch grabbed a vase and threw it against the wall. Everyone watched, but no one said anything. Without making eye contact, he walked over to Heid, bent over, and picked her up as though she were a sleeping child. He carried her over to the bed and laid her down upon it. He murmured a prayer under his breath, and covered her with a blanket.

Critch turned back to the group. "Tomorrow, we mourn. Then, we hunt Mason down and take him apart, one piece at a time."

They held a funeral for Gabriela Heid and the *Arcadia*'s crew the following day in the Rebus Station churchyard. The funeral had been planned before Heid's tragic death to free both her and her crew from the Collective's death warrants. The mission she'd taken to free her crew from the CUF's shackles had been courageous, even though he'd later learned the mission had served the ulterior purpose of killing Corps General Ausyar.

Despite his opinion on the latter part of the mission, he admitted there was a certain feeling of completion in having the *Arcadia* destroyed by its former armada. The loss of the *Arcadia* was a tremendous blow to the Campaign and a waste of a good ship. However, the CUF never would've stopped going after their stolen warship. Any peace negotiations would hinge on the ship being returned to the armada, and the three marshals had agreed that it was better for no one to have the warship than to give it back to the armada.

As for *Arcadia*'s crew, all, except Heid and the six killed in the Terran mission, were now considered dead in the eyes of the Collective. With fake identifications, they could go on to live full, free lives after the Campaign, assuming the fringe could break free from the Collective. Otherwise, Reyne knew that at some point in the future, one of the "dead" crew members would get arrested and undergo a DNA scan. They'd deal with the aftermath if and when that time came.

Right now, the crew was alive and free…except for Heid and the six, that was. He found it hard to stomach the irony of a fake funeral being held to allay any CUF suspicions, knowing that Heid's body lay enshrouded within the large stack of wood. Her body couldn't be seen, so any CUF spies watching would assume it was a symbolic funeral service since it was believed she was killed when the *Arcadia* was destroyed.

Since the five remaining crewmembers from the *Arcadia*'s final mission were also believed to be dead, they were watching via comm screens, along with the remaining crew at Nova Colony. The five knew of Heid's death, but Reyne wondered if someone had told the rest of her crew yet. He frowned. He should've checked.

Even without any crew in attendance, the funeral was huge, with hundreds of Terran colonists and torrents present. Reyne stood in the front row alongside Critch and Seda. Sixx, Boden, Hari, and several from Critch's crew stood behind them.

Reyne cast a quick glance over the crowd and swallowed the discomforting thought that if the CUF chose to bomb them now, the entire Campaign—along with Rebus Station—would be decimated in a single blast. He kept the concern to himself, as no one needed to dwell on *that* thought.

The funeral was conducted as a Terran service, despite Heid being Alluvian and having no religious affiliation. Heid lay, covered in dark muslin, disguised deeply within a pyre of traditional afromosia wood, the same wood used to make Terran whiskey barrels.

The minister gave a nice sermon, though Reyne thought he

droned on a bit long. Reyne knew Heid never would've asked for a service—she'd once told him she'd had enough rituals and procedures for one lifetime from her service in the CUF and serving the Founders. He found it more than a little ironic she was being forced to endure rituals even after her death.

Reyne was growing stiff from standing by the time the minister gave his final words.

"Gabriela Heid, marshal of the colonies, may you find the eversea."

The minister nodded in the trio's direction, and Reyne lifted a torch, as did Seda and Critch. The minister's apprentice carried a small torch over to them. The apprentice set alight each of the three larger torches, one by one, before hustling away.

The three men shared a quick glance before they stepped up to the pyre.

"May you find the eversea," Critch said quietly. He touched the torch to the pyre, and flames flickered to life.

Seda echoed the statement and touched his torch to another part of the pyre.

Reyne then repeated the same.

The pyre, lit at three places, erupted in flames.

The men stepped back as the fire engulfed Heid's body. Heat prickled Reyne's face, but he stood watch as the fire grew, and blocked any view of the body becoming ash.

He'd cared for Heid, but truthfully, he'd never had enough of a chance to know her. When they'd talked, it had almost always been about the Campaign and the colonies' independence. He felt sorrow that he, Critch, and Seda stood in to represent her when none of them truly knew her. He knew her crew would greatly mourn her loss, and he wished they could've been there in person for the funeral.

As it'd been for her, Reyne's crew was his real family, and as their captain and father figure, he hoped he never had to see off any of his crew on their journey to the eversea. Especially Throttle. His greatest fear—the fear that woke him every night with a cold sweat—was that Throttle would die before him. Anguish squeezed his heart.

Seda glanced down at his wrist comm, and then looked to Critch and Reyne. He nodded for them to follow. Reyne gave one final parting look toward Heid. He turned to Boden and Sixx. "I'll meet you back at the ship," he whispered, before following Seda from the churchyard.

When they reached the sidewalk, Seda spoke. "The CUF has a new corps general, and he's on his way down here right now to negotiate a peace treaty. He'll be here within the hour."

CHAPTER 20

RENEGOTIATIONS

Rebus Station, Terra
Seda

SEDA HAD a feeling of déjà vu as he waited in his chambers for the new corps general to arrive. Critch sat in the same chair as he had last time. The only difference was, this time, Reyne sat in a chair next to him.

"Thanks for staying," Seda said to Reyne.

Reyne gave him a look. "When this is done, I'm still leaving. What happened last night doesn't change my mind."

Seda gave a tight nod. He couldn't blame Reyne. Where Critch was vengeance and Heid had been determination, Reyne was conscience. Seda was the negotiator, a neutral hand to lead the colonies to freedom. It was his failure that they'd hid the blight from Reyne. And Seda feared that failure would come to haunt him. Seda had resources and understood politics, but Critch and Reyne understood military strategy. They needed each other if the colonies were to achieve a true independence.

And what Seda saw today was that they were falling apart. First, Heid's death. Now, Reyne's imminent departure. Without strong, united leadership, how could they maintain a unified fringe?

Feeling the weight upon his shoulders, he took a seat at his desk to monitor the CUF envoy. They'd pulled up outside the stationhouse and were now entering the building. Seda turned on the video for recording in case this new leader was even worse than Ausyar. Seda nearly chortled. Someone worse than Ausyar? Couldn't be possible...could it?

He stood as the CUF officer entered the room with his entourage. The man was easily twenty years younger than Ausyar, and an Alluvian where Ausyar was a Myrad. That distinction alone gave Seda hope. Alluvians were *much* easier to talk to.

"Hello, Stationmaster Faulk. I'm Corps General Barrett Anders." The man held out his hand.

Seda gripped his forearm. "It's a pleasure to make your acquaintance, Corps General. I recognize you from when you accompanied your predecessor here to discuss negotiations." He motioned to the two empty chairs, and they each sat.

"Yes," Anders said. "It was unfortunate more progress could not have been made that day."

"I agree," Seda said.

"Before we begin," Anders began. "I'd like to offer you my condolences for Gabriela Heid. Gabi and I studied at the academy together, and I was shocked to learn of her choosing the colonies over the Collective." He paused. "In the Forces, it's considered an honor to go down with one's ship. At least she had that."

"Yes, she had." Seda's eye twitched when Critch muttered something behind him. "She was an admirable marshal and respected captain. Her death was a waste and completely unnecessary."

"The Collective Unified Forces code of conduct would have me disagree." He sighed. "But I'm only human, and I mourn her death, nonetheless."

"As do we all," Seda concurred. "Let me offer my condolences for the death of Corps General Michel Ausyar and the crew of the *Unity*. What happened was truly tragic."

"It was," Anders said, leaning in. "It took me some time to convince myself that something as truly evil as the blight not only still existed, but that there were those who still found value in its application."

Seda forced himself to not glance in Critch or Reyne's direction. He focused on the corps general who sat before him. "As I said. I found the event to be a tragedy of the highest order."

Anders eyes narrowed. "I've found myself in a dilemma when it comes to you and to what happened about Rebus Station on that fateful day. If you didn't condone the use of the blight, then I can only assume that you have no control over the torrents, and negotiations with you are then null and void." He lifted a finger. "However, if you did condone the use of the deadly fungus, then I can only assume you find no value in the life of your enemy, and I worry how many innocents could die in your quest for independence."

Inside, Seda raged. He hated the concept of the blight. Worse, the knowledge of his role in its latest application sickened him. If there had been any other way to level the field, he'd have taken it. But there hadn't been another way.

Seda eyed Anders. "I can assure you that any negotiations mutually agreed upon in this room will be adhered to by the colonists. And, I can also assure you that I treasure life very, very much. After all, my respect for life is why I've dedicated my life—

and finances—to ensuring colonists can live as fully and freely as citizens."

Anders rubbed his hands together. "I believe that brings us to the matter at hand. I have notified Parliament of my intentions to negotiate with you a peace treaty that mutually benefits citizens and colonists. Parliament has not authorized these negotiations, but I'm here. I believe if we reach a fair and equitable solution, Parliament must consider it."

"I would like to think they would as well," Seda said, though he doubted it.

"I have given great thought to what you discussed during the first meeting, and wish to begin with your original proposal. I'm much younger than my predecessor, so forgive my lack of experience. However, my entire life, I have seen turmoil between Myr and Alluvia and the colonies. If there's something I can do to end that turmoil, I will do it." He paused for the briefest of moments. "You want Parliament to accept your declaration of independence as a legal document. You demand that all the colonies be recognized as free and independent from the Collective, with trade opportunities."

Seda nodded. "That is correct."

"However, you must understand that Parliament's hands are tied to some extent. If the colonies all broke from the Collective, the economy would collapse. The Collective stands on the shoulders of all six worlds. I'm sure you can imagine the impact that suddenly losing four of those worlds would have. The loss in taxes alone would drop the Collective into a full-blown depression."

"I understand," Seda replied. "Conversely, the colonies have been asking for equality for decades, and rather than listen, Parliament has only instituted more restrictions. We've reached an impasse. I see no alternative."

Anders raised a finger. "Try this option. What if all colonies without space docks were to become independent? Colonies with space docks would remain within the Collective, with each having the ability to propose their own path to independence to Parliament after ten years."

Seda laughed. "Give us the fringe, and you take the fringe stations. Without space dock capabilities, you'd be effectively isolating every colony from each other. No. The only way the Collective will keep the fringe stations from becoming independent is by finishing what they started—by bombing them or blighting them."

"Planets with no stations would certainly serve no good to either the Collective or the fringe." Anders lips curled upward the smallest degree. "If the colonies are to be free, then the Collective must have assurances the space docks will welcome Collective traders. The fringe stations must maintain open trade with Myrad and Alluvian traders alike, with guaranteed annual minimum quantities and negotiated fair rates for each planet, along with an option to reevaluate trade agreements after an established duration."

Seda watched him for a moment as he tried to determine if Anders was playing him or truly looking out for everyone's best interests, which he found impossibly hard to believe. "Your proposal sounds fair, assuming the trade quantities and rates are agreed upon by both parties. Likewise, I'd like to see Myr and Alluvia retain certain trading with colonists."

"That is assumed. You see, my family owns a fishing business on Alluvia. It's a small business, but we get by. Most of our stock is catfish, which isn't highly prized by Alluvians. Exports to the colonies have kept my family's business alive, so I understand the value of trading going both ways."

"Fried catfish is a personal favorite of mine," Seda said.

"I'll be sure to bring you some the next time I'm on Terra," Anders said. "Speaking of Terra, I also assume any Terran trade agreements are inclusive of Faulk Industries. As you get new fuel production facilities up and running, the Collective would receive a percentage of production units at a fair rate."

If Seda's group of companies was being singled out during peace treaty negotiations, taking the juice from the Collective had proved to have a greater and faster impact than he'd expected. He felt no need to hide his smile. "Absolutely."

Anders leaned back like he'd just finished a large meal. "I believe we could come to a fair and equitable arrangement, one that negates the use of any continued physical force on either side. However, I'm sure certain concessions will need to be made."

"As long as those concessions don't derail the integrity of the treaty, they are open for discussion. All colonies must be independent. That is a non-negotiable truth."

Anders nodded. "I will personally deliver this proposal to Parliament. Now, in regard to the stolen CUF property, the *Arcadia* is clearly no longer an issue, but the *Matador* remains."

"Unfortunately, I'm afraid the *Matador* had mechanical issues. Without the needed expertise, the ship's caretakers chose to disassemble her for parts. By the time I learned of her demise, there was nothing I could do."

"I see. That's unfortunate." He pushed to his feet. "I believe we've covered what we need to for one day. My final proposal is, we have a cease-fire until this verbal understanding can be discussed with Parliament. And, I need your assurance that biological warfare will never be used again. The blight is abhorrent, something that never should've been created in the first place."

Seda stood. "I will do everything in my power to prevent the use of biological warfare. You have my word we will not be the aggressors, but should there be any actions taken against any colonist, we will do what is needed to protect the colonies' interests."

"Understood, and I give you my word the CUF will not show aggression during this time of cease-fire. However," He raised a finger. "You should know that I intend to launch a full investigation into the murder of the *Unity*'s crew. I will bring the perpetrators to justice."

Seda prayed that Critch was betraying no emotion on his face. "Agreed. I would expect nothing else."

The pair clasped forearms.

Seda walked the corps general to the door. "I can only hope the progress we've made today will not be quashed by those who don't have the Collective's or the colonies' best interests in mind."

"As do I," Anders responded.

Before Anders left, Seda paused. "A moment, Corps General."

Anders motioned for his staff to leave the room, and Seda turned to Critch and Reyne. The two marshals didn't look pleased, but they exited the room.

When only the pair remained in the room, Seda eyed Anders. "This went exactly as you intended, didn't it?"

Anders glanced around the room. "Is this on the record or off the record?"

Seda walked over to his desk and turned off the recording. "Off the record."

Anders gave a look like he didn't know whether to believe Seda or not. "I believe it's the inherent nature of any colony to become independent once it reaches a level of self-sustainment. However, I am also aware we are all currently interdependent upon one another. I'd much rather be exploring new solar systems than policing systems that don't want me there. Perhaps, if the colonies were free, we could all move forward, citizens and colonists alike, into new endeavors and discover something innovative and exciting." Anders tilted his head toward Seda. "Until we meet again."

Anders departed, leaving Seda staring as the door closed behind the military officer.

Hari returned first. "So, is he on our side?"

Seda thought for a long moment. "I have no idea."

CHAPTER 21

CREW CHANGES

Torrent Headquarters, Terra
Reyne

CORPS GENERAL ANDERS led the fleet from Terra that same day. The *Unity* remained in orbit, a ghost ship filled with the dead. Until the CUF sent disinfectant teams with the fungicide, the ship would continue to linger above Terra.

Reyne had waited all day for the CUF fleet to depart Terra's orbit to safely make his own departure. By then, it was well into the night, and he, Sixx, and Boden decided to wait until morning to leave. He slept restlessly throughout the night, anxious to get out and search for Throttle. By sunrise, he was running through pre-flight sequences.

"How's she look?" Sixx asked as he entered the bridge.

"Everything's in the green," Reyne said. "Once Boden gets here and runs through engine checks, we're good for departure."

When Sixx didn't speak, Reyne turned to find him leaning against the wall, thinking.

"You okay?" Reyne asked.

Sixx looked up. "Are you sure you're good with us leaving during the Campaign?"

"Yes," he replied, "Unequivocally. The Campaign is over, at least for us. It's up to Seda to handle the politics. Besides, it's long past time we focus on finding Throttle and Qelle. After that, we'll see which direction the wind blows us."

Sixx gave him a sideways glance before agreeing. He pushed off from the wall. "I guess I'd better say my goodbyes."

Sixx headed off the ship, and Reyne shifted his concentration back to his pre-flight checks. While he was scanning systems, a small ship docked next to him. A Chital, if he wasn't mistaken. He'd never seen it around before. Something tickled at his curiosity, and he paused the scans and casually strolled outside and toward the other ship.

The Chital's door opened when he'd reached halfway between the two ships, and a pretty woman—though looking quite disheveled—stepped out, holding a hand of a little girl who clutched a teddy bear in her other hand. The woman looked around, and when she saw Reyne, she called out, "Hey, you. I need a wheelchair over here. Can you find me one?"

His jaw slackened, and his entire body froze. He couldn't even breathe. One step moved him forward, then the next. Soon, he was running up the ramp and into the ship. The ship was so small it only had a cockpit area with living space around it. His gaze fell instantly on the black-haired woman in a long gown, unstrapping her seatbelt. Disappointment stung—Throttle was blond and would never be caught dead in a dress—until he realized that the way she moved was too familiar.

"Throttle?" The question came out like a plea.

She turned, and Reyne nearly collapsed.

"Reyne!" she said and held out her arms.

He ran to her and held her tight as he murmured, "I thought you were—I thought—doesn't matter. I love you."

"I love you, too, Dad."

He didn't miss the fact that she'd called him "dad." She'd never called him dad to his face before. His eyes welled with tears that soon streamed down his cheeks. He sniffled and wiped his eyes. "Come on, let's get you out of here."

He lifted her from her seat and carried her off the ship and into the fresh air outside. The ship had smelled beyond ripe—the air purification system clearly needed work. Though, he realized when he carried Throttle, she hadn't showered in a long time.

"What happened?" he asked.

"Long story," she said. "I'll fill you in later. Right now, I could really use some *real* food. Shane had only stocked cavote bars and blue tea on the ship." She shivered. "Ten crates of cavote bars and twenty gallons of blue tea."

When he stepped onto the dock, he saw Boden standing there, staring, slack-jawed.

"Hey, Tren," she said with a smile.

Boden continued to stare. "You're..." He rushed to her

Reyne grimaced. "Don't just stand there. Go get her wheels."

"Oh. Okay." He ran back to the *Gryphon* to grab the spare wheelchair they kept in back to use whenever Throttle's regular wheelchair went in for seat replacement and tune-up.

"You're okay," Reyne said. "I can't believe you're here—and you're okay." He frowned. "Why are you here? Why didn't you go to Playa?"

Throttle winced.

"What's wrong?" Reyne asked, suddenly worried.

She shook her head. "Nothing. Just phantom pains."

He frowned. You haven't had one of those in years."

"I'll tell you later." She nodded toward the woman and girl standing off to the side. Reyne had completely forgotten about them. "That's Bree, and that's Lily." The little girl waved when Throttle introduced her.

Boden returned with her chair. Reyne set her down, and Boden immediately embraced her. "I thought I lost you," he said softly, though loud enough Reyne could hear.

"I'm not that easy to get rid of," she said, still holding him.

He pulled away, but left a hand on her shoulder, and she laid a hand over his. After a moment, he began to push her toward the hangar. Bree and Lily tagged along.

"Why didn't you go to Playa? That was our RP," Reyne said.

"I figured Sixx would still be on Terra."

He furrowed his brow in confusion. "Why would it matter if Sixx was here?"

"Because Lily is Qelle's daughter."

Reyne stumbled before finding his pace again. "And Qelle?"

Throttle's attention had been pulled away, and Reyne then noticed Sixx jogging over.

"Well, I'll be a wombie's uncle." Sixx grinned broadly and rubbed her shoulder. "Hey, kiddo. It's good to see you."

"Good to see you, too, Sixx," Throttle said.

Sixx lifted his wrist comm. "Wait. You're wearing a dress. I need to get a picture of this."

She hid her face. "Don't you dare."

"You're Jeyde Sixx?" Bree asked.

"I am." He squeezed Throttle's hand, and then stepped over to meet the newcomers. "I don't believe we've met."

"No," she said. "Throttle has been telling us about you. I'm Bree."

Sixx took her hand and kissed the top of it. "It's nice to meet you, Bree." He stepped back and got down on a knee and gave Lily a big smile. "And who might—" His smile dropped at the same time he lost his speech.

Lily hugged her bear closer to her.

Several seconds passed. Then, he lifted his hand and brushed it across her cheek in the gentlest of manners. "You have your mother's eyes."

▭

"And there you have it," Throttle said. She polished off her third bottle of soda, and Birk jumped up to get her another.

After giving the new arrivals a few hours to bathe, get new clothes, and eat, it was late in the day. When they'd emerged clean and refreshed, Seda's lounge had filled with people anxious to hear their tale. Critch and Birk arrived first, with Birk staying glued to Throttle's side. Reyne didn't fail to notice that Boden stayed glued on her other side. Seda and Hari came directly from the stationhouse when they heard Throttle had arrived. Several of Critch's crew trickled in throughout the afternoon.

Throttle and Bree led the tale, with Lily providing a remark now and then. Sixx never took his eyes off Lily, and the little girl kept eyeing him with suspicion. The girl was timid, but she had a strength to her. Reyne wondered what sorts of abuses she'd seen while under the same roof as a slaver.

Throttle still had stain in her hair, though it was a lighter shade now that she'd showered. But Reyne noticed a change in her eyes that he found far more profound than the abrupt change in hair color. In her eyes, it seemed she'd aged decades. She was no longer the young woman he'd last seen on Spate. He'd seen the same change in fresh recruits before and after battle. Throttle had seen hell, and she'd be forever different.

Sixx turned to Throttle. "He won't get away with it," he said sternly, and everyone knew the "he" Sixx spoke of was Axos Wintsel.

"You're damn right he won't," Throttle said. "We'll both make sure of that."

"We'll *all* make sure of it," Reyne said, "Together."

"Together," Bree chimed in.

"Yeah," Lily added, and several chuckles emerged, though there was little humor to be found in the situation.

Seda stood. "You're all welcome to stay here as long as you need. Now, I need to get back to work." Hari stood also, and left the room with Seda.

Birk jumped up like something bit him. "I'll be right back," he said, and he rushed out of the lounge.

Throttle grinned, and then shook her head.

Boden whispered something in her ear, and she laughed. Then, Boden sobered. "I missed you."

"I missed you, too," she said.

Birk came running back into the room and practically fell onto his chair. "Throttle..." He sucked in a deep breath, as though trying to inhale courage. "I have to ask you something."

Reyne cringed. *Oh, please don't propose to her.*

Birk reached into his pocket, and Reyne wanted to cower. *He's going to propose.*

Boden looked like he was about to choke.

Birk pulled out a keycard and held it up to her. Reyne audibly sighed, and he noticed Sixx raise a brow in his direction.

"Critch gave me the *Scorpia*," Birk began. "But I'm no pilot. I've got no crew. It's a great ship. I think we'd make a great team. I guess what I'm saying is, will you fly the *Scorpia*?"

She looked at him. "You want me to work for you?"

His eyes grew wide. "No! Not at all. What I meant to ask if you'd be my partner. Fifty-fifty. The *Scorpia* would be half yours."

Reyne's heart became a rock slamming inside his chest at that moment.

Throttle looked equally shocked. "You're offering me the *Scorpia*?"

Birk nodded. "Yeah. I mean, we'd share it and all, but I think we'd make a good team."

"You said that already," she said.

He was about to say more, and then clamped his mouth shut.

Throttle spoke slowly and steadily. "That's a big offer, Birk. A really big offer. Let me think on it tonight, okay? I'll have an answer for you in the morning."

Critch stood. "It's good to have you back, Throttle." He motioned to his guys. "My crew's bugged you enough for one day. That especially includes you, Birk."

"Okay," Birk said. "I'll stop by later." He stood and kissed her full on the lips.

As Birk, Critch, and the rest of his crew headed toward the door, Reyne noticed the anger in Boden's eyes. While Reyne was none too pleased with what Birk had just done, he made a mental note to caution the younger man to look out for the temperamental Alluvian.

"Hey, Critch?" Throttle called out.

Critch stopped and turned, while the rest of his crew exited.

"If I fly the *Scorpia*, am I on your crew, or Reyne's crew?" she asked.

"Mine." Critch shot a look at Reyne, who gave him his best glare. "Uh. Both crews."

Throttle narrowed her gaze. "After the Citadel run, you made me an offer. Does that offer still stand?"

His eyes narrowed. He glanced at her legs, and then back up at her. "Of course."

She nodded. "Thanks. I'll let you know in the morning."

The lounge cleared out, leaving only the *Gryphon*'s crew and the two newcomers, though Lily had dozed off nearly an hour ago.

Reyne turned to Throttle. "I know you like Birk, and he's offering you quite an investment opportunity, but—"

"But you don't want me to take it," Throttle said.

"Of course I don't. I hope you know the *Gryphon* is yours if you want it."

"I thought I was going to get the *Gryphon*," Sixx chimed in.

Throttle smiled at Sixx before turning her attention back to Reyne. "You have to trust me to make the right choice. This is not a decision I'm going to make lightly."

Throttle and Bree shared a look, and then Throttle spoke. "There's a couple of other things I want to talk with you guys about."

A couple of other things. Reyne looked at the woman and child, and suspected he knew exactly where Throttle was leading him.

"I'll cut straight to the chase. I'd like to recommend Bree to join the crew."

Reyne looked at Bree and back to Throttle. "We're not in the charity business. Every crewmember plays a specific role."

"Bree is a jack-of-all-trades," Throttle said. "Really, you should've seen how she handled things on the Chital."

"Sorry, darling," Sixx said. "But I'm the jack-of-all-trades on this crew."

Bree lifted her chin. "I also am pretty good with first aid." After a second, she shrugged. "Medical skills were a necessity taking care of people who worked under a Wintsel. I've seen more cuts and broken bones in a year than you've seen in your life."

"I'm not sure about that," Reyne said.

"Not sure about giving Bree a chance, or about seeing more cuts and broken bones than you've seen in your life?" Throttle asked.

"Both," Reyne said.

"At least think on it," Throttle said. "I got to know Bree and

Lily really well on the flight here. And I know Bree would fit in great on the *Gryphon*."

"And you want Lily to come on board, too," Reyne said as a matter of fact.

"You brought me on board when I was less than half her age. Lily is smart, and not afraid of anything."

"And she's another mouth to feed," Reyne said. "Not to mention the *Gryphon* is still an active torrent ship that could find itself in a battle at any moment."

"It wouldn't be any worse than what she's seen already," Bree said.

"Then she's likely traumatized and needs professional help," Reyne countered.

"She's coming with us," Sixx said.

Reyne turned to Sixx "What did you say?"

"She's coming with us." He took a deep, calming breath. "I know Qelle would want me to take care of her like she was my own, and that's damn well what I'm going to do."

Reyne threw his hands out, knowing when he was defeated, but also not feeling entirely bad about it. "I've raised one daughter on that ship. Sure, why not yours?" He turned to Boden. "Are you going to bring one next?"

Boden held up his hands in surrender and shook his head.

"Then it's settled," Reyne said in a calmer voice. "Bree, you're on the crew." When she smiled, he held up a finger. "On a probationary basis. And Lily..."

He noticed the little girl was awake and now watching him. He found himself smiling at her. "Welcome to the crew."

▭

After another restless night, this time worrying about what decision Throttle would make, Reyne was up at dawn and waiting for his crew. He didn't prep the *Gryphon*. Instead, he waited until Throttle emerged from her room.

When Birk followed, Reyne's heart plummeted.

She saw him and turned back to Birk. "You head down. I'll catch up."

He kissed her, and Reyne decided he'd let Boden at the scrawny kid.

Reyne scowled at Birk as he walked down the hall, whistling. He turned back to Throttle. "He's a pirate," he grumbled as he walked alongside her.

"He makes me laugh," she said.

Reyne swallowed. "You made your choice."

"I did."

He found a lump in his throat. "I can't fly without you."

"You're a good pilot," she said.

"Not as good as you. And that's not what I meant."

She sighed. "I know." She stopped pushing her chair forward. "I have to do this. I don't know how to explain it, but everything up here"—she waved a hand by her head—"is jumbled right now. I need different scenery until I get it worked out. I know that doesn't make any sense."

"It does," he said. "After the Uprising, I was in a dark place. I couldn't go back to where I'd been before because I'd become a different person. I felt lost. That's when I decided to become a fringe runner. Not for the paycheck. I did it so I could get away from everyone and everything I knew before."

"Yeah," she said so softly he barely heard the word.

He knelt. "I don't want you to go. Believe me, if I could get you to stay and still live with myself afterward, I would. But that's me being selfish, and that wouldn't be fair to you. I know this is something you've got to do, so I won't stop you. But if you ever change your mind, or if you ever just need me, you know you're never alone. No matter how far you fly or what you do, I'll always be there. You know that, right?"

Her eyes shone with wetness. "Yeah. I know."

They hugged, this time even longer than when they'd found each other at the docks yesterday. When Reyne pulled back, he sucked in a deep breath. "So, when do you head off in the *Scorpia*?"

She hastily wiped a tear from her cheek. "Not for a couple weeks, at least. Remember when I popped down to Broken Mountain, not long after the Citadel was freed?"

"Of course."

She shrugged. "Well, Critch made an offer to me during that time. He offered to pay for surgery to repair my spine. All I had to do was sign up for his crew." She shrugged. "Flying the *Scorpia* counts." She grinned. "Guess he got screwed on that deal, huh."

Reyne shook his head and smiled. "Nah."

The pair headed down to the dock where Sixx, Boden, Bree, and Lily were already waiting.

Boden smiled. "You're coming with us."

Throttle winced. "No. I'm staying."

Boden's face fell before he collected his emotions and forced a small nod.

Bree came over, bent down, and hugged Throttle. "Thank you."

Lily stared at Throttle with a look like she was on the verge of tears. "You're not coming?"

"No, honey. I have to stay here to have my legs fixed."

Lily ran and jumped onto Throttle's lap. "Will your legs work the next time I see you? They won't hurt anymore?"

Throttle nodded. "We'll dance when I see you again."

Lily buried her face in Throttle's neck, and they hugged. When Throttle tickled her, she laughed and jumped off.

"I'll send you a message every day," Lily said. "You better call."

Throttle lifted her left arm. "As soon as I get a new wrist comm, I'll call you all the time."

Lily giggled, and then nestled against Bree.

Sixx came over. "I can't believe you're ditching us for a pirate."

She shrugged. "It's a step up from flying with a professional thief."

He smiled and rubbed her head.

Throttle's face grew serious when she looked at Lily, and she spoke in a low voice. "Axos will never stop searching for Lily."

"Let him come," Sixx answered with nonchalance. A dark smile crept up his face. "I can promise you that he won't be in one piece when I'm finished with him."

Reyne chimed in. "If he comes after us, it saves us the time having to hunt him down."

She looked at him, confused.

Sixx grinned. "We're going after Axos, kiddo. We should have a good head start by the time you and Loverboy leave Terra."

Her lax jaw closed, and she pursed her lips. "You better leave some of that Myrad vig for me to finish off."

Reyne eyed Sixx and nodded to the *Gryphon*. Sixx squeezed Throttle's shoulder. "See you soon, sis."

As Sixx headed to the ship, Reyne focused on Throttle. "Watch yourself around here. Mason's still out there, and he holds a pretty big grudge against Seda and Critch. Who knows what he'll try next."

"I'll be careful," she said.

"When you get tired of Birk, you know there's always a pilot seat on the *Gryphon*."

"I know, Dad." She pulled him down to her, hugged him, and kissed his cheek.

When he came back to full height, he soaked in her face, never wanting to forget that moment.

"It's okay. You'll see me again soon."

He shrugged. "It's an awfully big universe."

She smiled. "But it's a small galaxy."

THE COLLECTIVE

The Collective is comprised of six terraformed planets in nearby solar systems within the Milky Way galaxy. The Collective is controlled by the dual leadership of Alluvia and Myr. Only those born on Alluvia and Myr are given legal status as citizens, while all others are considered colonists and receive fewer privileges. The Collective views colonists as means to achieve gain, and their pressure is driving the colonies—the fringe—to desperate actions.

MYR is a silver-rich, water-rich citizen world with idyllic islands. Myr was the first settled planet in the Collective. Myrads have argyria and take great pride in their blue-hued skin.

ALLUVIA is a water-covered citizen world and home to First City, the Collective's largest city. Alluvia was the second settled planet in the Collective, and has the highest gravity of all Collective worlds. Alluvia has thick cloud cover and frequent storms.

DARIOS is the most naturally habitable world and provides much of the Collective's food supply. As such, it's heavily regulated by the Collective. Its fringe station is Sol Base, which had been hit by the blight. Since then, the CUF has maintained a chokehold on Sol Base.

PLAYA is the furthest world from Alluvia and Myr. It has low gravity and freezing temperatures. Its fringe station is Ice Port, which was destroyed by the CUF. The Collective believes Playa to no longer be of value, now that its fringe station was destroyed. Unknown to the CUF, the torrent headquarters is here, located at Tulan Base, which has its own space dock.

SPATE is a desert-like world and has the largest fringe station, Devil Town, known for its massive indoor garden. Without a stationmaster, it is seen as neutral territory.

TERRA is a battle-scarred world, where much of the Fringe Liberation Campaign now takes place. Its fringe station is Rebus Station. Terra, the planet nearest to Alluvia and Myr, stands between the citizen worlds and Darios, making it a key planet in the Campaign. The torrent headquarters on Terra are located within Seda Faulk's secret retreat and space dock.

SPACE COAST is an asteroid belt outside Collective control and home to smugglers, pirates, and other outlaws. Its fringe station is Nova Colony. The CUF initiated a blockade when the Fringe Liberation Campaign began.

GLOSSARY OF TERMS

ABYSS: *Term used to describe people and ships lost in space, presumed or known dead.*

CHIMESUIT: *Blue, armored space suit worn by dromadiers. Named for the chime-like sounds the suit emits.*

CITIZEN: *Free person born on Alluvia or Myr.*

COLONIST *aka Fringe: General population in the fringe. Considered impure and lesser by many citizens.*

COMM: *References communications sent/received, as well as personal communication devices.*

CUF: *Collective Unified Forces (CUF). The Collective's military led by Corps General Michel Ausyar.*

DRIFT: *Slang term, meaning to die or to kill. E.g., "I drifted him with a single shot to the head."*

DROMADIER: *Soldier in the Collective Unified Forces.*

EM FIELD: *Short for Electro Magnetic Field. On-ship technology to produce artificial gravity.*

EMP: *Short for Electro Magnetic Pulse. Weapon employed by the CUF to disable ships.*

EVERSEA: *A term referencing the space frontier. An Eden.*

FOUNDERS: *Secret organization of citizens and colonists who steer the Collective's actions using ulterior methods. Believed to have gone defunct after the War.*

FRINGE: *Refers to the tributary planets and colonists under Collective control (Darios, Playa, Spate, and Terra), as well as the Space Coast.*

FRINGE LIBERATION CAMPAIGN: *The official term for the war taking place between the colonies and the citizen worlds.*

FRINGE STATION: *A trading outpost with space docks. Located in the planet's largest colony.*

JUMP SPEED: *fastest speed at which ships currently travel. Requires jump shields to protect crews from hydrogen radiation poisoning from high, faster-than-light speeds.*

LOGGER: *Waterlogged "puffy" person addicted to seasoned water, i.e. water seasoned with sweet soy.*

PIRATE: *Outlaw who raids ships and smuggles contraband.*

REBUS RECLAMATION EFFORT: *The initiative, led by Seda Faulk, to force the CUF from Rebus Station.*

RILON: *Extremely durable yet flexible metal used on most hulls, weapons, and tools.*

RUNNER: *Interstellar postman and transporter. Fringe runners commonly smuggle blue tea or sweet soy.*

SOLAR SAILS: *Large flexible sails on ships used for long-haul space travel.*

SPECTERS: *Elite torrent space fleet. Many specters were pirate ships prior to the Campaign.*

STAR SWARM: *Tsunami of space garbage/debris pulled into an asteroid's gravitational pull.*

STRETCH: *Playan colonist with low-g mutations. Extremely tall, with respiratory and heart defects.*

SWEET SOY: *Highly addictive drug, often mixed with water.*

TENURED: *Indentured servant. Tenured are often tricked into servitude.*

TORRENT: *Colonist rebel who fought in the Uprising twenty years before the Fringe Series takes place.*

UPRISING: *A revolt by the fringe colonists against citizens of Alluvia and Myr for equal rights.*

VIG: *Derogatory term, referring to a small, smelly rodent found on Spate.*

VOICELESS: *Tenured who have had their vocal*

cords destroyed because they broke laws or attempted to escape servitude.

The WAR: *War between Alluvia and Myr. The War ended with a truce and the creation of the Collective, as well as initiating the push for colonizing other worlds for resources.*

WOMBIE: *Mutated, slow-moving Spaten colonists who have developed a camel-like ability to store water. Have extremely low IQs.*

ABOUT THE AUTHOR

Rachel Aukes is the award-winning author of over thirty novels, including *100 Days in Deadland*, which made Suspense Magazine's Best of the Year list. She is also a Wattpad Star, her stories having over seven million reads. When not writing, she can be found flying old airplanes over the Midwest countryside and catering to an exceptionally spoiled fifty-pound lapdog.

Join Rachel's spam-free newsletter to be the first to hear about new releases: www.rachelaukes.com/join

ACKNOWLEDGMENTS

With extreme thanks to my editors, Stephanie Riva and Laurel Kriegler, for helping bring this story to life. This book would have never seen the light of day without you. And, thank you to Walter Scott for the generosity and early feedback. Also, huge thanks to my husband for the support, even when (especially when) he gets pulled into a brainstorming session on the many ways to kill someone in space. Most of all, thank you, my readers, for your messages, cheers, and enthusiasm.